GUARDIANS' BETRAYAL

WHAT HAPPENS SEVEN YEARS
AFTER ADOPTION

JOHANNA VAN ZANTEN

Print ISBN: 978-1-54390-931-9

eBook ISBN: 978-1-54390-932-6

Cover design by Bookbaby

Editing: The Word Is Out Writing Services

Published by Bookbaby 2017

PROLOGUE

Bernice had prepared Abbey and Shayla for the possibility of seeing their mom in the casket and that she might look different. When they entered the auditorium, she saw a crowd gathered at the front around the casket. They walked up: Bernice first, followed by the two children, and Wanda as last. The casket was open.

Nora's face was made up with too-beige foundation, lipstick on her closed mouth, her hair shiny and spread out like a cloud around her face – not at all like she had been in life – and she was dressed in a white blouse, vest and jeans. Her black leather bike jacket was displayed on a stand nearby. Bernice studied the girls' faces, but saw no reaction at all. She wondered what actual details they were taking in, looking overwhelmed by the commotion around them.

The children didn't appear to know anybody in the crowd, except Uncle, and their broad smiles and tight hugs told Bernice they were relieved seeing him there. That seemed to be the sign for others and several of Nora's friends drew the girls into embraces – although the girls didn't give any sign of recognizing them – blowing their boozy breath into their little faces while mumbling "you, poor child" and "so sorry". A few others assured the children that Nora was family, while weeping unabashedly.

Bernice wanted to pull the children away from their greedy arms and leave the hall with them, but for the sake of the children and propriety, had not done so. The pungent-sweet smell of alcohol and the sounds of weeping adults filled the hall. She had never before witnessed a spectacle like it.

The crowd found their seats, the loudest weepers on the front row. Six-year old Abby sat next to Bernice in the third row behind foster parent Wanda, who sat on the second row with Shayla. The children did not cry at all. When the pastor invited speakers to say a few words, Shayla walked up to the podium with Wanda as her sentinel next to her.

She started reading a letter to her mom with a voice as clear as a bell for all to hear, her face barely visible over the lectern. She declared her love and promised she would never forget her. Bernice, like all others in the crowd, was moved to tears by that heartbreaking, unusual performance of this brave adult-child: Already a grown-up at age ten.

Then Shayla left the stage, walked over to the open casket and laid the pages of her letter at her mother's feet, and started walking back with Wanda to her seat, when Abby ran up to Shayla and threw her arms around her waist, holding on for dear life. Together they walked to the seats on the second row, where Wanda sat down between them, an arm around each child while the officiating minister talked on the podium about Nora, obviously without having known her, judging by his platitudes.

Bernice couldn't help noticing that most of Nora's friends were very intoxicated or high on drugs, or both, all dressed for the occasion in biker's garb – types she would cross the street for. Several strolled in casually during the service that had started at 10 a.m. – way too early for these night owls – as if they had stopped the party for a minute to attend the funeral. A man of about 35 with shoulder-length hair in the front row continued weeping loudly throughout the service, held upright by his mates on each side.

After a brief word from the pastor, the ceremony ended and the grieving man calmed down. The crowd got up and dispersed throughout the space and onto the reception area. Bernice sought out the weeping man when he was standing by himself, upright, away from the crowd; he smelled like somebody had baptised him with a bottle of cheap whiskey.

"Excuse me, I couldn't help noticing you're very sad. May I ask you, how you are related to Abby and Shayla?" He stared at her, not understanding. She tried again: "I heard you say 'Your mother is family'. What is your family connection? Are you Nora's brother?"

He looked at her, his gaze moving up and down taking in her image, and concluding she wasn't part of the clan, he answered with a rough and hostile voice. "No, I just know her. Who're you?"

Bernice explained she was the family's social worker, but before she could finish her sentence, he walked away with a look of disgust on his face. It slowly dawned on her: The man meant the word 'family' in the crime family sense. She had known about Nora's suspected affiliation with a local gang, but the actual reality was so much different than in the movies and her imagination. It didn't stop her from approaching others to find out if they could be of help to Abby and Shayla, as everybody moved slowly into the reception area, adjacent to the court yard with the parked hearse and the waiting casket inside it.

The girls nibbled on the food. "Look, Bernice, my favourite fried chicken," commented Abby. Bernice estimated that out of the roughly 50 attendants maybe three other adults had been sober and clean: Uncle's neighbour who had arranged the funeral, the pastor, and one of the fathers of the girls' siblings – as she came to know him after the eulogy.

This man in his forties came up to her pushing his two reluctant teenaged sons ahead of him. "You're the social worker?" They had a brief chat; Bernice took his information, while the brothers spoke with the girls. Abby didn't give any sign of recognition, but Shayla slowly remembered their names. The conversation had been awkward; they didn't know what to say to each other. "Well, we'd better go now," said the father. "We have a long drive back to Edmonton ahead of us."

After the brothers had left, Shayla pointed to a dark-haired man with a pony tail standing to the side, close to the exit, and said: "That's my dad." Bernice had seen him come in late during the pastor's opening words and disappear somewhere in the back rows. Looking back at Wanda – occupied with Uncle's neighbour – Bernice decided she wouldn't pass up this chance, and with the girls in tow, moved through the noisy crowd towards the man.

She offered her hand explaining who she was. His hand was shaking uncontrollably. He hugged his children and stayed for a few moments with them at a table in the reception space, desperately trying to have a conversation, but the girls didn't know what to say either. His face was very pale and his whole body appeared jittery – badly in need of a hit, she concluded.

She gave him her business card. "Please, would you call me, and would you come to the foster home for a visit? I'd like to make sure that Shayla and Abby will know who their father is as they grow up." One moment he was there, the next he wasn't. He had left the hall without saying goodbye.

"Where's my dad?" Abby asked.

"I think he left. I guess he wasn't feeling well and had to go, but I've set up a visit after the weekend; he can call you too, and when he gives you his number, you could call him. You'll see him again." That seemed to satisfy her. After the girls finished their lunch, Wanda took Shayla and Abby home.

———

After the adoption, talk about their biological family stalled. Tom didn't want to hear about their history, afraid he would like the girls less with more information about their birth parents' sordid background – as if the sins of the fathers spoken in actual words might infect the children. The girls didn't ask anymore and moved on with their lives.

Tom left most adoption decisions up to Bernice. In special circumstances, adoption policy allowed a social worker to adopt foster children, on the condition that another office conducted the suitability interviews and criminal checks at arm's length. It so happened and finally, Bernice and Tom got the nod. The usual steps of many – happy – visits to get acquainted as a family followed and they all really clicked; the girls were delighted to have a dad and a mom, and gladly played older sisters to Tom and Bernice's preschoolers, Jonathan and Daniel. Although briefly sad over leaving Wanda's home, the sadness evaporated when Wanda continued visiting and became an occasional sitter and an enduring family friend. Things had moved along swimmingly.

CHAPTER 1

The frantic bark of a dog from her cell phone alerted Bernice while in a meeting with her supervisor. After a furtive glance at its screen to identify the caller, she tried to put Shayla off by not answering. She was in the middle of case supervision and had some difficult decisions to make: To remove or not remove. Although Bernice was a seasoned social worker and knew what to do to keep children safe, policy demanded that she'd consult with her boss on those important case decisions.

Located in the central interior of the liberally-minded pacific province, opinions nevertheless could vastly differ on her team in this conservative-minded mid-size town. That made team discussions all the more interesting, although the provincial laws and the mission set by the minister would ultimately determine a social worker's course of action.

Her team leader nodded. "I don't mind if you get that. Our kids are important to us. You never know what the problem might be. I'll just check my email for a few minutes."

Bernice needed to clarify: "It's Shayla; I could get it later. Her emergencies are not really that urgent," she replied with a smile on her face, but left the office anyway. Out in the hallway, she said more sharply than she intended: "Yes, Shayla. What do you want?"

"Oh, Mom. Why don't you pick up the phone right away! I don't have a ride and the bus left already. Can you pick me up?"

Kids could be so unreasonable; she replied: "I'm working. Didn't you say you'd go with Anita and her mom to the mall to buy a present for Friday's birthday party?"

"No, they backed out on me; like, her mom has no time, or something. I think Anita doesn't want me to come anymore; she probably left already for the mall, taking Ellen with her instead of me, and didn't want to tell me. So just like her!"

Shayla's voice had that whining quality Bernice had been unable to break her from – a habit that Shayla discovered as a good tool years ago. With Bernice, she usually got what she wanted. At seventeen, Shayla was an industrious and reliable young lady. Bernice was grateful and considered the whining only a minor flaw compared to other children Shayla's age that could be a hand-full. She made her own voice sound calm and reasonable.

"You don't know that." She couldn't withhold a sigh. This was so typical of Shayla, to take something at its worst. "Did you see them leave together and getting into her mom's car?"

"No, not really."

"Now, then! See? I haven't finished working yet. See you at the front entrance in thirty minutes or so, maybe a bit later. Wait there for me, okay?"

She wondered whether the time had come to let Shayla know the facts of her birth mother's accident seven years ago. Her daughter wasn't a child anymore that needed full-on protection, now that she was going to be driving a car. Bernice rejoined her supervisor; they continued their case consult, assessing the strengths and weaknesses of the parent in the case under scrutiny.

***

Forty-five minutes later, Bernice slid her car along the curb at Shayla's school. During the ride home they discussed how soon Shayla could own a car, needed to foster her independency. It was essential to her status, Shayla said, and to speed up the process she proposed: "Well, why don't you let me drive you until then, Mom? I can do it; you know I've had my driver's licence for a long time. I could drop you off at work and like, use the car to drive myself to school every day, and pick you up later from work. You can trust me." Looking at her with big, trusting eyes, stirred Bernice's heart.

"No way. You're a very reliable girl, but still, I wouldn't want to be dependent on you. What would I do when I can't get away and have to stay later to finish up with an emergency? No, it won't work. You'll just have to ride the bus like everybody else, or wait for me to give you rides, sweetheart! Until you can afford your own vehicle." She petted her daughter's hand resting on a knee.

"Like, you don't trust me – obviously. But Mom, I almost saved up enough to start looking for a car, you know. My babysitting job's been great. Like, last weekend the Johnsons stayed out till, like 2 a.m., big bucks for me. And their friends, you know them; Darla is her name and her husband is Chris, really cool people. They asked me for next Saturday for their game night at the Johnsons' place. With my job's dollars, I might buy a car in a few months."

Shayla worked part time as a cashier in a grocery store in addition to baby-sitting for a number of befriended families.

"Wonderful, I can't wait." Bernice didn't see any sign of her daughter noticing the tinge of sarcasm in her mom's voice; reading those subtleties of interactions was not one of her strengths. She was the kind of girl that parents wished for, the kind of girl who genuinely liked and got along with young children, including her little brothers. She played with them and was mothering them, as if she was born to it.

Of course, that's exactly what she had been doing all of her life; as their social worker, Bernice had been well aware of the girls' past, and was careful not to misuse Shayla's gift for mothering. She would let Shayla only babysit occasionally for her youngest darlings, when their regular after-school caregiver fell ill and Shayla was available – for a fee of course.

Driving along in silence, Bernice's thoughts were stuck on her daughter's nature. She'd often wondered whether Shayla's overly serious and pessimistic view was a result of her early history. To be fair to her, that willingness to care for others perhaps might just be Shayla's character and personality. She dismissed that thought immediately; it seemed unnatural for a girl that young to take on that much responsibility. It must have been by force majeure.

Shayla called her friend Anita. Bernice listened to the one-sided conversation. If she wanted to know more, she could just ask – Shayla didn't keep any secrets from her – although she was able to fill in the blanks. "Hey, what's up? Have you heard from Ellen?"

Anita answered.

"Sure, that's alright," Shayla replied, without much conviction.

Anita spoke.

"If nobody can give us a ride tomorrow, we can always, like, take the city bus to the mall after school. Okay, I'll come tomorrow."

After arriving at home, Shayla grabbed the home phone to save her own cell phone minutes, and continued talking– as usual – for what Bernice estimated was close to an hour. Bernice's was raised differently. The black wall phone in her parents' home located in the living room was meant for brief conversations only, as its use was expensive and closely monitored by her parents. She envied Shayla's habit of endless phone conversations and that ability to use the phone so freely. Her thoughts went back to her teenage years, that time full of promise before university and marriage. Where did the time go?

Just then, her two boys interrupted her thoughts with their loud screeching, embroiled in a fight over a video game received as a gift from their grandparents. "Give that console! Give it to me, give it!" Daniel screamed, embroiled in a tug of war with Jonathan in the living room.

She wasn't happy with video games taking the place of playtime outside, and believed it led to anti-social behaviour – the main reason for limiting the boys' game time to one hour after school. She hadn't expected the side effect of that nasty competition between her sons, but hadn't found a remedy, if there even was one.

Bernice hurriedly left the kitchen area, calling out: "One more argument and I'll take it away for the rest of the week; your consequence for not sharing." She stood in front of the boys, who had stopped tugging at the control pad, and stared in disbelief at her for a few seconds, until they found the words to argue.

"But, it's my turn and I don't want to play with him, he always wins and he cheats!" said Jonathan, the youngest, his voice high-pitched and his face flushed. Two years younger than Daniel, he had trouble keeping up.

"Would you really want me to treat you like a baby and let you win, or do you want to get better at it?" replied Daniel with reason – the territory of an elder brother.

"You could let him play by himself," suggested his mom.

"But what fun is that?" whined Daniel.

"It's fun for me," yelled Jonathan. After giving each other dirty looks for a few seconds, the two boys soon settled back into a two-player game, allowing her to return to what she was doing in the kitchen.

She called out to Abby playing with her Barbie dolls in her bedroom down the hall. "Will you help me get dinner going?" At thirteen she really was too old for Barbie dolls, but her baby girl still liked them a lot. Bernice didn't like the unnaturally endowed dolls she thought primed girls for an unrealistic body image, but she'd been unable to stop the Barbie exposure. One of her regular child care helpers had passed on her own box with dolls to Abby; she didn't have the heart to deny the gift.

Throwing the dolls carelessly in the large box Abby happily replied. "Sure, what are we having for dinner?" She was really into cooking lately.

"I thought we'd make some soft tacos; that's easy to make and we've got everything for it. You can make a salad. I bought some great heirloom tomatoes yesterday on the farmers' market and the adults can add some cheese from the local goat farm."

"Gross, Mom. How can you eat that stuff; it stinks."

"Well, sweetheart, it's an acquired taste, as they say. You might start liking it when you're older. Just don't put any on your plate."

It was about time for Tom to come home; Bernice looked at the wall clock and saw that Tom was late – again. He had recently been promoted to the position of senior manager at his real estate company, supervising twenty realtors. Tom had felt gratified by the big promotion; he was an ambitious man. She knew he also was a responsible man and a great father to their boys and their adopted girls, although wasn't not fond of having a bigger family than originally planned, but she had to give it to him: He had adjusted seamlessly to the situation.

They had explained to others that Shayla and Abby came to them by choice. Things were good – so far at least, except she thought he was working too hard. The prospect of being alone with Tom later that night made her warm all over, imagining their little tryst. Anticipation was half the fun.

That night, Bernice made an effort to get the kids tucked in early. If Shayla was still up, she would be in her own room on the lower floor, doing her homework, or watching TV in the family room. Bernice saw Tom leave for the master bedroom, where she joined him a few minutes later.

When she entered the room with its corner fireplace and the large flat screen TV, Tom was watching the game on top of the bedcovers, leaning back against a stack of pillows, dressed in only boxer shorts and a beer in his hand. She snuggled up to him and started nibbling on his earlobe, and whispered in his ear: "Hey, lover boy. Want to have a little fun?"

Tom laid his hand on her thigh, pushing it gently, but firmly, keeping his distance. "Maybe some other time, if you don't mind, sweetie. I'm really tired, had a rough day and wanted to watch the hockey game. You'd take a rain check?" He lovingly patted her thigh, making her well-developed upper legs tremble, bent towards her and kissed her forehead. She had always hated that patronizing, distancing gesture. She was doing the math: They hadn't made love in two months. Maybe she shouldn't be put off so easily.

Her hand crept up towards his chest to stroke his torso while throwing her leg over his, pressing her body against him, caressed his ear with her tongue – generally good tactics for turning him on. Not this time: Tom ignored her, and his body did too. When her hand started to travel, he grabbed it, holding it tightly into his. "Not tonight, I said," he repeated coolly, his blue eyes trained on the TV screen. He looked handsome, even athletic with his bare torso and brush cut, turning greyish at the temples.

Bernice withdrew, settling back on her side of the bed with a tiny squeeze in her heart. She couldn't help herself and started planning, instead of accepting: "Sure, sweetheart, if that's what you want. Maybe we could go out this weekend, see a movie or so. Spend some we-time. What do you say? I'll ask Shayla what her plans are; she might stay home with the kids."

Without looking at her he replied in a carefully maintained, neutral tone. "Sounds like a plan."

She looked at him next to her in their matrimonial bed – Tom only interested in the game – and the letdown hit her full-on grabbing her heart, and squeezing it a bit more. She consciously started breathing in and out, slowly and deeply, to get it to leave her chest; it worked and she regained her calm and rational train of thought. Things always seem to be about the kids, or work. Was something wrong, was she missing something?

She inspected her life for a possible flaw and couldn't find any. They had renovated the house to make more space for two extra kids. Back then, she already realized they needed to safeguard their private time as a couple and to make that private relaxing possible, they had installed a Jacuzzi for two in their bathroom. Tom agreed with her on the renovation, and on how she raised the kids; he generally agreed with everything she did. Bernice was happy with him; Tom was a good husband.

She smiled; yes, they were good together. No, nothing was wrong; she just should be patient. She crawled under the cover and started reading her book, a novel about a woman and her daughter trapped in another country, kept hostage by her husband and his relatives. Soon she felt her eyelids becoming very heavy; the noise from the hockey game faded away. She was asleep.

CHAPTER 2

S hayla impatiently dropped the sunglasses back into the bin. No, that's not what she wanted. She strolled down the aisle, and moved deeper into the jungle of the department store towards the ladies' clothing. A large advertising sign hanging from the ceiling on small chains told her in large retro-style lettering that the new spring collection had arrived. Yes, she would like that: A new outfit always made her feel better.

She let the clothes' fabrics – much thinner and silkier than the sturdier winter fabrics – slide through her fingers. The new colors pleased her. She took four pairs of pants and two tops from the racks, took them to the fitting rooms, saw no attendant, went inside an open cubicle and tried on the clothes. She would be the first one to have this style of pants, wide and silky, flowing and soft; wearing them made her already feel older and very feminine.

Her image in the mirror reflected a sophisticated and tall young woman. The style fit her more mature body better than the skinny pants of the last few seasons. She looked at the price tags: Not quite her budget. Shayla opened the door a crack and looked over towards the make-up and perfume department, where she saw Anita and Ellen browsing, and considered asking them for a loan, then rejected that idea immediately, and closed the door. They earned less money than her; she had two jobs.

She didn't want to look needy anyway; they already thought she was a loser. Whenever the three of them were together, she felt like the odd one out and searched for evidence that Anita didn't like her as well as she liked Ellen. No, she wasn't going to ask them for anything; she could manage fine without them. She'd rather die, or steal.

She took off the pants, quickly put her own sweatshirt over top of the thin, silky sweater, tore off the tag and threw it under the bench, left the empty hanger behind in the change room and hung the rest of the clothes on the rack by the exit. She walked over to the cashier where she paid for the pants, then quickly left the area. She joined her friends at the nail polish display.

"Let's go for a mocha-chino," she said in an attempt to get them out of that area and moving on to the food court, away from the store. They agreed. At the coffee shop she took out her finds. "Hey, guys, look what I bought; what do you think?"

"Yeah, great pair of pants; those are those wide-legged pants, aren't they? I like those a lot," Anita said, while Ellen replied coolly: "Sure, they're nice."

Shayla stuffed them back into the bag. She did not mention the thin sweater underneath her own clothes.

At home, she undressed, carefully folded her new top and put it away in her closet between her other tops. In awe over her own cleverness, a delicious pride rose in her. Who would believe she had the guts to get her new pant-top combination in this ingenious, cheap way? Really a steal! She smiled, thinking about tomorrow night – especially the prospect of a party to go to, looking like a million bucks. She would be meeting that guy, Eric. She's had a crush on him since last year, but after his transfer to another school, she didn't have many chances to meet him. She had not told her friends; they would only make fun of her. She couldn't take that risk.

She knew she wasn't the only girl who liked him, and that stupid girl had been so dumb to let it be known to all who wanted to listen that she really liked Eric. That loser bragged about seeing him, making up the story of going out; Shayla knew for a fact it was a lie. She hadn't told her mom about Eric either, although Shayla told her everything; since she had got a mom, she really liked having somebody to tell things to, but this was different. She hardly remembered her real mom. No, she should say, her *birth* mom, because Bernice was her real mom now.

She pushed away thoughts about those confusing times of long ago; a pervasive sense of weariness always surfaced. She didn't want to remember and forced her body and soul to turn into a different direction – away from those feelings that she couldn't even name. That's all in the past: Her life was good now. She changed her mind and decided to show her mom her purchases. She went upstairs with the clothes over her arm. She got the result she was hoping for.

"That's a wonderful combination, Shayla, well done. You've got good taste. Was it expensive?"

"No, Mom, not as much as you'd think it would cost; it was a really good deal."

"From which store did you get it?"

"I got it at Sweet Jane; they really have good sales on."

"Why don't you put it on and give us a show, after dinner? Your dad would love to see it."

"Sure, I'll give a show, when Dad is home."

After dinner, Shayla showed off, all dressed up in her new duds. Checking herself in her full-size mirror, she concluded that putting her hair in a casual up-do gave her a remarkably mature look. Dad was home this Friday evening, watching a game in his den and he even came out of his sanctuary to watch her together with her mom. Shayla played it up with a savvy, sexy attitude that – by the looks on their faces – surprised them. She swiveled her hips while firmly planting her feet one before the other, like the models she'd seen on the cat-walk on TV.

"Hey, honey, come here for a minute," her mom said and drew her close, giving her a tight hug. "I think you look beautiful and I love you. I'm proud of you for making good choices and being so smart with your money. Good for you."

"Thanks, Mom, love you, too."

CHAPTER 3

Later that Friday evening, Tom wandered into the family room where Abby and Bernice were playing a game of Scrabble. Shayla had gone out to her party and the boys were playing their video games – in harmony this time.

"Bernice, I need to finish up some work at the office for a deal I might soon close, a million-dollar home in the lakeshore area. The prospective buyer wants to see more data of comparable properties. Do you mind? It would take me a few hours to get that material together."

"No, I don't mind, Tom. If you need to do that, I trust it's important. I'm staying up for Shayla anyway, so see you later then."

"Okay, honey, but don't wait up for me. You had a busy day yourself." He came over and gave her a kiss on the top of her head. Then he kissed Abby on her cheek. She threw her arms around him and hugged him tightly, hanging off his neck. "Love you, Daddy."

"Night, kids, be good for mom, boys."

"Yes, Dad!" they responded in unison, too busy with the games to stop and hug him. Bernice assumed she wouldn't get to see him again that night, and sighed.

The next morning, Tom and the boys went to Jonathan's Saturday soccer game – their usual boys' bonding time – always with a lunch of their choice afterwards, probably low-grade, fatty and overly-salty food, followed by something sweet and full of empty calories. That was completely fine with Bernice. The rest of the week she'd make the effort with home-cooked, healthy fare while Tom cooked one meal a week with help from the boys, as agreed when adding the two girls to their family. It had to be something easy, as he wasn't into cooking, so that turned out to be steak and pre-cooked French fries from the oven with a salad most times. The boys were getting quite good at constructing salads.

At first it had been tough going for all; both Shayla and Abby were emotionally withdrawn – although very polite – needing time to thaw out emotionally; that's how Bernice described it to her friends and family. Prior to Tom agreeing to adopt the girls, she had an extensive, ongoing discussion of several days with him, until they came to an agreement in the end. She recalled shards of that conversation.

"What do you mean with 'frozen'; they look quite alright to me," Tom had commented.

"That's just the honeymoon phase as we call it, when the kids want to be liked and won't show their not-so-sweet sides, their anger, their fears, and their strange habits. Trust me, every child raised in neglect has some weird behaviours – adaptations to the old life. While they're trying hard to be good, we won't get to see those. There may come a testing phase too to see whether we're really going to stick around for them – warts and all."

"What makes you think that will happen at all?"

"Wanda told me she saw some problems already, but overall she thought Shayla and Abby were good kids. When their trust has grown, they'll eventually show us more of that negative stuff, at least that's what I expect."

"Oh, how do you know these two are not exactly what they showed us on the trial visits?"

"Well, I don't know for sure, but in my work I've seen that happen with adopted parents and their newly placed children. It might take a year or more, but after the kids get used to their new caregivers and relax, start being themselves, their true personality comes through and you get an idea what the future might be, living with them long term. Quite a few adoptive parents throw in the towel at that stage, not prepared to deal with the reactivity. Adoption breakdown, especially hurtful for abandoned kids."

She remembered feeling strange, as if educating a new foster parent, but knew she should give Tom all of the facts, to be fair to him. Back then, she had added: "I personally don't care what the girls will be like in the future. All I know is that Abby and Shayla need to know we are not ever going to leave them, even when things get difficult. I for one want Abby and Shayla to be able to trust us, to make up for what they didn't have. That's why I want to give them a permanent home. Don't you want that for the girls?"

"Of course I do!"

After a few days of talking and Tom wavering, he finally relented. "We have no girls and Shayla and Abby would make us a perfect family: Two for you and two for me. I'm sure we can handle anything together. Besides, they deserve to have some happiness after what they've been through." That's how it was settled: They became a family by choice, and if it was up to Bernice forever – regardless of what might happen in the future.

In the beginning, it was very strange to get two halfway grown-up daughters without any experience what girls are like. They were truly strangers to each other, although Bernice had an advantage over Tom with a few months of case management and frequent visits, much more than the required one visit every three months – simply too little time to get to know a child. Within record time, they became the girls' adoptive parents.

With space to breathe this Saturday, Bernice shook her head in amazement. Things had really unfolded beyond expectation, but had it been that long ago? It seemed like yesterday that she got those timid, sweet girls into het car to take them home for good. Where did the time go? She wondered what time Tom got home last night and how well he had slept on the couch.

CHAPTER 4

When Tom got home around three in the morning, he took a shower to wash off the alcohol in his body. Still on adrenaline from his clandestine adventure and fully alert, he decided to work on the company Internet site. It would be most inconvenient to face Bernice, so he chose the path of least resistance, seeing nothing wrong with that strategy; it worked out fine for him. He had a good handle on his home life and work.

Contrary to his laissez-faire approach, Tom's desire for Marla told a different story. Recalling the last few hours he spent with her, a sense of breathlessness lingered. He wondered what the beautiful, young Marla he had just left behind at her home, saw in him and why she so much enjoyed his company. He estimated her about fifteen years younger – at the very least, possibly maybe even more – although it was hard to tell women's ages these days. He was no spring chicken, although he prided himself on still having all his hair, and the bit of graying gave his appearance quite a distinguished look, like George Clooney; at least that's what the women at his office told him.

"I could help you with those property searches, if you like," she had offered. He had gratefully accepted, and thought his offer for a drink afterwards more than justified.

"Thanks so much for the work you did, Marla. You're a lifesaver. Can I offer you having a drink? You deserve it, spending your Saturday evening with work and your boss." He made his voice sound gentle, casual, and non-threatening, so she'd be able to back out easily, but she hadn't.

They had a few drinks. To his surprise, Marla turned out to be a smart lady and funny to boot. They enjoyed each other's company. Tom's pectorals lifted, his spine straightened in her company, and his step quickened; the years melted away, reminding him of his earlier days of vim and vigor. She talked about her life. He had asked her why she was still single and found out she was twenty-five.

"You know, Tom, it's really difficult to find a suitable guy with some ambition who's willing to commit. At my age, most men want the adventure, play around, and get bored with you when they reached their goal – the hook-up. I'd rather stay single than catching a guy who turns out to be a jerk. I really intend to make something of my life."

On saying their goodbyes in front of Marla's home, she bent over to him; her kiss was delicious, a slight brushing of the lips, barely touching. He felt encouraged when she leaned into him, lingering, and he kissed her back, full and long, drawing her body into his with his right arm, aware of the slightness of her torso. Instantly aroused by the idea of more to come, he let go of her, slightly breathless. After she quickly left his car and slammed its door shut, he drew in a deep breath of air. She disappeared into the apartment building, leaving Tom behind, dizzy. For a few seconds the thought of a heart attack flashed through his mind, which dissipated, when he caught his breath.

Tom was a patient man; he found that most situations sorted themselves out. He felt that hasty actions often caused unnecessary complications. Bernice often teased him about this character trait; his British phlegmatic personality, she called it. Yes, he was raised not to wear his heart on his sleeve, to be in control of his emotions at all times, and to preserve some measure of calm in any circumstance.

He had that from his father, who had it in turn from the British public school, which was a private school, contrary to what the word meant on this side of the Atlantic. At those strict schools, the instructors teach students how to speak perfect English, to extinguish any lower class accent. His old man still corrected Tom's use of language, which annoyed Tom to no end, but he kept his mouth shut. Avoiding conflicts had become his specialty. He knew better than to argue with his father about projecting oneself into the right class; *his* goals were altogether different. The only class on this side of the world was wealth, and his own goal was just that.

A sudden suspicion shocked him into reality. Marla said she wanted to get settled. Was his status and wealth the attraction for her? But he couldn't be with her that way; he already had a family with kids, for god sakes. He would have to leave Bernice! Is that what she was after? Most of his friends were divorced, or already in their second marriage. They complained about their wife taking it all – referring to the family assets – and leaving the ex-husband to pay child maintenance throughout their children's childhood, and sometimes even beyond, through university. It seemed unfair.

Letting that realization sink in, he went on line and cruised the Internet in a haphazard search on the word 'divorce', until he saw a website that dealt with division of assets in divorce. Just for the hell of it, he entered it, rationalizing he wanted to see what people were so perturbed about. Until now, he was satisfied with how well his and

Bernice's registered retirement plans fared with the allowable maximum contributions – the glitch had been the 2008 financial crisis, but he managed a virtually complete recovery from that dip.

In spite of the slow real estate market, he was doing well in his business, as he specialized in the relatively untouched high-end sector. Looking forward to add Bernice's reliable government pension, he concluded the family was financially okay, even with the two extra children acquired along the way. Maybe he was jumping the gun thinking this far ahead, but he definitely didn't want to lose half of his assets with a divorce and a new start with Marla – or another wife – but how in the world had he ended up here anyway?

Tom had to be honest with himself. He had a wife who was too busy to make time for him, too busy to really see *him* and admire him, and to tell him *he* was her life. He simply didn't have the heart to tell Bernice about his reluctance about taking on Shayla and Abby, when all she talked about was the emotional crisis of the girls, painting a disastrous future of eternally bouncing from foster home to foster home – the girls past adoptable ages – if *they* wouldn't adopt them.

Last Sunday, he had commented to her at the breakfast table in a tone of voice that made her look up. "How come you're never giving me a manicure or a haircut anymore? It's been several years. I just loved getting that special treatment from you."

She just had looked at him in disbelief, eyes wide, and a smile curling at one side of her mouth. "Truly? You're serious?"

He choked back more comments swallowing hard, thinking back with nostalgia about that special era with her without any children, feeling like a jerk for even bringing up the grooming. She was busy enough as it was and he did not want to add to her load. They each went on with what they were doing with an uncomfortable silence between them after his comment.

He hated the boys' screeching about video games and got really tired of Shayla's dramas, but Bernice was preoccupied with the welfare of the children and with teaching them the right things. He tried to help as much as he could and felt guilty when he was skipping out. He admired and loved Bernice and her commitment to their children, but in spite of his love, the funny and exuberant, spontaneous and lovely woman he fell in love with, had disappeared. He just had to accept that and move on emotionally, be mature about it, find a way to carry on and keep it together. His love for her had nothing to do with Marla: both kinds of love could surely coexist.

The next morning was Sunday and nothing was out of the ordinary, although he felt fundamentally changed, somehow. After breakfast, Shayla and her mother discussed the party she went to; the other children had left the breakfast table. Tom listened to it for a bit and heard Shayla say after the last pancake had disappeared, "Mom, I've got to tell you something,".

"Yes, what is it, sweetie?"

"I met someone. His name is Eric. I like him. I think I've got a crush on him. Like, I danced with him a couple of times and I didn't know what to say; he must've thought I'm stupid or something. You know, he paid a lot of attention to Ellen. Like, I think he's more into her."

Tom kept quiet, but noticed Bernice's intense stare at Shayla as the girl was rather casually chatting about it, and he suspected Bernice was already torn inside with worry. "Is that right? I'm sorry sweetheart, but with boys you never can tell from the outside how they really feel. He might feel different inside, but afraid to show, for fear somebody might embarrass him by confronting him with his feelings." Hearing this, he wondered whether Bernice meant this for him or for Shayla; he left for his den downstairs without anybody noticing.

CHAPTER 5

A typical Sunday meant a family activity and that day, the whole Harrison clan left for the community pool. Bernice, the organizer and mediator, found it more difficult each Sunday to get everybody to agree on the activity – all children adamant on pursuing their different interests. Tom was often absent due to showing homes to prospective buyers. Shayla wanted some time on her own and asked to be relieved from the joint recreation to hang out with her friends on the weekend. Bernice would like to devote more time for her exercises, well aware that she neglected herself in the last few years.

Bernice and Tom agreed that it was time to let the family trips go and that each parent would accommodate the children's individual activities going forward. Today was their last official family event together. After spending some time splashing about and chasing each other in the community pool, they all had a warm-up in the sauna, before going home and doing their own things.

Bernice wanted to work off the pound-per-year she had gained over the last decade without paying too much attention to it, until now. Before giving in to her desire to relax after the family swim, she decided to go for a walk and share some time with Tom, who had already disappeared to his den. When she entered his domain, he closed the laptop lid.

"Hey, Tom, want to go for walk with me? Shayla's home; the boys are fine. It'll be light for another few hours; let's take advantage of it. I was thinking doing the Lakeshore trail. Come on, what do you say?"

Tom looked up in surprise. "Sure, sounds like a good idea. I could use the fresh air." It sounded like an automatic reply and not so much a conscious decision, but she'd take it; beggars can't be choosers.

———————

They walked in silence side by side on the trail, each at a different pace, Bernice straining to keep up with Tom's long legs taking one step for her two. After a while, Tom asked, "Is your life the way you want it to be, honey?"

"I'm fine, a bit tired, that's why I wanted to go for a walk, to wake up my energy. Where does that question come from, Tom? No, I'm not completely happy. I'd like us to do more things together, just you and me. I miss you. I also want to start yoga lessons. Maybe you could join me."

"Bernice, no offense; it's just a question. I noticed you seem tired and sleep a lot; maybe there's a reason for it?" Tom glanced at her and then looked straight ahead.

She slowed down her pace and grabbed his arm. "What do you mean with there's a reason? Of course there is; I do a lot of work, but now the kids are getting older and don't always need us anymore. What are you saying? You already have an idea? Are you suggesting a vacation?"

26

Forced to walk slower, he looked at her with a sincere face: "I don't know that I can make time; I'm pretty busy at work. You know that I have to be on call as a manager. What did you have in mind?"

"Oh, I see. You're kicking it back to me. I'm saying I want to do less with the kids and more with you. This is just an example: I would like to take classes in ballroom dancing. There are several clubs in town that offer classes and they put on events, where we could practice. I'd love it if we gave it a go."

His face said it all when he replied: "I can't commit to anything in particular on a regular basis. Dance class? Really? I've got two left feet. It'd be torture for you; might have to wear steel-toed dancing shoes, honey." They both laughed. Stuck in her usual mode of operandi, she put her formidable persuasion skills to work; Tom relented and agreed to join her. They would try dance lessons.

Returning home after a refreshing walk, they found Shayla in a mood in the living room, sprawled across the couch with her laptop, silent and brooding. Bernice exchanged a glance with Tom, who rolled his eyes. She sat down with her and asked whether she would like to talk about it, but Shayla said she wanted to be alone and escaped to her bedroom.

Not used to this treatment from her daughter, Bernice went to the adjacent kitchen and made herself a snack: carrots stick, celery, and dip. With an audible sigh, Tom retreated to the family room, where the boys played their games and Abby played with her Barbie dolls. Standing by the stairs, Bernice listened in on the children's conversations with Tom. The boys didn't want to talk to him, absorbed in their video game. On his way to the den, Abby asked him to play house with her and the dolls. Tom would usually oblige. Bernice heard his excuse.

"Hey, Abby, honey, I think I'll pass today; I'm a bit tired; I'll take a rain check, is that okay?"

"Oh, really? Too bad, Daddy; how come you're tired? You're never tired."

"I worked late last night, honey. I'll be in the den, if anybody wants me." She heard Tom quietly close the door. He probably went on his laptop, she guessed, and wondered what was so important to pass up playtime with his daughter, and to whom he sent his messages.

CHAPTER 6

On Monday morning, when everybody in the Harrison family was getting ready to leave for school or work and in a hurry, Shayla called out from the bottom of the stairs. "Mom, look at this, come here, quick. I got an email from my sister!"

"What sister? I'm coming." Oh no, the computer. Bernice's heart skipped a beat and her knees were unwilling and weak running down the stairs, as if she had spent an hour in the lotus position. She permitting Shayla to have her laptop in her room after she worked two summers and paid for the laptop herself; it was her pride and joy. She had made sure Shayla was aware of all the pitfalls of Internet communication. Panting, she entered Shayla's room and saw her bent over her laptop.

"Look here, it's from a girl with my birth mom's last name, Michaud. I'm sure she's my sister; I remember her name from my adoption Life Book, don't you remember? Can I reply and say yes? Please, please, pretty please, Mom? I want to know what she wants. I'm so excited, please, Mom?"

"Sure, sweetheart. I always wanted you to have a connection with your relatives. If I were you, I'd be curious too. I also want to know

29

what happened to her, and to your two brothers. Do you remember them?"

"Not really. It's so long ago."

"Yes, of course; you were so young. I wonder how old your sister would be now; let me think. She must be 26 now. But you're going to miss the bus; you need to hurry up; check "accept request" and then get going, please."

"Right. I hope she replies. Mom, I'm so excited! I sort of forgot about my brothers. Like, they were so much older and I really don't remember their faces." Shayla checked the box and accepted her new "friend." Bernice tried to be patient and empathic with Shayla, but was rattled enough by the sister's attempt to reconnect to call Tom at work, as soon as she arrived at the office. She told him about Anna's friend request. A fullness settled in her stomach, as if she had eaten and drank too much and soon would vomit.

"What are we going to do, Tom? We can't stop this contact, but I sure would want to set some solid boundaries for the relatives."

"You should find out what they do now," was his logical reply.

"Yes, I need to get an update on what they're like. I'd hate to see our girls be dragged down by their biological family. They're doing so well." Her voice became less frantic as she spoke; Tom had that effect on her.

"Could you legally stop them from seeing the girls?" The question a realtor would ask, she thought, gratefully.

"Thanks for that question. As a matter of fact, we as the parents have every right to decline all contact with birth family, if we wanted that. I told Shayla she could accept the friend request. What are you saying, Tom? Is that what you want to do? She'll be mad as hell."

"I'm not sure. I need some time to think about that, Bernice. It's shocking, after seven years of silence. I wonder what's bringing this on. I'm in the middle of something at the office here; can I call you back?"

She heard voices I the background. "Sure. Or could we meet for lunch? We've got to come up with something before we get home today."

"I am sort of swamped today, but I could do an early lunch around 11:30. Can you get away?"

"I'll make sure I get somebody to cover for me. See you then. Oh, but where?"

"At the diner around the corner from me, what's it called, Next Stop or something.

"The First Stop. Okay, see you there."

That morning Bernice was unable to concentrate; she felt a migraine coming on. The office lights bothered her and she turned them off; sometimes she could stave off a full-blown attack by staying in the dark. Bursting to tell her best buddy at work about Shayla's sister, Bernice convinced her first line of support and confidante in all matters of the heart – Angela – to take a coffee break and the two disappeared into her dimly-lit office.

Angela suggested that a suddenly reappearing relative could destabilize the family, and setting boundaries was important. "If you and Tom are too strict in your responses and Shayla still feels loyal to these relatives, she might rebel. Blood ties are strong."

"Her reactions were surprisingly intense; I can't be sure which way this whole thing will turn. We'll just have to be careful. Thanks,

Angela. It's great to talk to someone who understands; Tom is sometimes so dense about the girls."

She decided to meet Tom at his office, in case he would dawdle, or call her with an excuse for cancelling lunch. She left the office early and arrived at Tom's office ten minutes before the agreed time.

———

She wasn't hungry and her head still hurt when she entered the lobby, announced herself to the pretty secretary at the front desk, and asked for Tom.

"Yes, Missus Harrison, of course. I'll let him know you're here."

Tom came out to the front immediately. As soon as they walked outside, Bernice started talking. She thought immediate action was called for, as things might get out of hand. Tom wanted to sleep on it and decide later. He seemed less upset than Bernice about the whole situation, although she expected him to play it down in his usual approach. They discussed what kind of boundaries were called for and decided to allow Shayla to email Anna, but for any visits they would need more time to decide.

"We'd have to know more about Anna Michaud. Does she have a criminal history, and what's her connection to their mother's world? If that's the case, I can't allow ongoing contact: Any connection to Nora's gang would mean trouble."

"I don't know much about that history and I don't want to know. It's your call, dear."

They arrived at the restaurant. Tom opened the door for her, a habit of his, but this time Bernice was struck by the gesture, appreciating his gallantry. They both ordered the lunch special – soup and a sandwich – and discussed the particulars of how they were going to deal with the conundrum of a long lost relative showing up in their daughters' world. By the end of lunch, they had agreed they would tackle the discussion with Shayla together that same evening, and get her agreement on contacting Anna only under specific conditions.

———————

At the end of the business day, Bernice got a call from Tom: "An assignment came up that I needed to deal with. Could you please deal with Shayla without me? I'll be coming home later than usual."

"Okay, fine, but I'm not happy about it. I thought we'd deal with important situations together. You're abandoning us." She felt anxious; her stomach had not settled and her headache became worse. Things were getting off track.

"Don't dramatize, Bernice; I'm sure you can handle this by yourself."

Tom was less friendly than usual, and her anger rose as her migraine intensified; she questioned why she always had to do everything. She decided to turn her energy to more urgent matters and for once, look after her own needs. She quickly left the office and drove home; her headache had become a full-blown migraine. She needed to lie down. Her stomach was rebelling. She hated her life at this very moment.

———————

A couple of hours later, Shayla arrived home from school. Bernice heard her running back and forth many times between the laptop in the living room and her other activities elsewhere in the house, until she apparently got a reply on Facebook from Anna and called for her mom. While the sharp pain shot through her head with the effort of calling out, Bernice finally replied. "I'm in the bedroom."

"You'll never believe what happened, Mom," Shayla said breathlessly, bursting into the bedroom.

"What, honey? Could you please keep your voice down? I've got a headache. What's up? Did you hear back from Anna?"

"Did I ever! Mom, she wants to meet me and Abby, and she has two girls of her own and a husband. She's seeing my dad and he lives in the same town, just a two-hour drive away from here; he also wants to see us. Omigod, this is so excellent; like, I will have my dad back!"

Bernice had to swallow hard before she could respond; her lunch was rising up, as if somebody had hit her hard in the stomach. Gently, she said, with a noticeable tone of reproach in her voice: "But Shayla, you have a dad."

Shayla stopped abruptly on the spot. With a barely audible voice she spoke. "I know that. I mean my other dad. You know what I mean."

Her usual self control was weakened by the migraine and Bernice's autonomous nervous system took over and made her lips say the words she would regret as soon as spoken: "Shayla! You're talking about a man, who was never a dad to you in real life, not even one day, no more than a father in name, a sperm donor."

Shayla's face said it all – eyes wide, mouth in a grimace, her brows pulled together in a frown. A minute later she recovered and she spoke again, half-crying: "Mom, aren't you happy for me? I don't understand what you're saying."

Trying to regain control, aware she had responded purely from emotion, Bernice took a deep breath. "Sorry, honey, that didn't come out right. I thought you were pretty happy with Dad and me; aren't you? Please, listen carefully to what I'm saying. There was a reason why you needed to come into foster care and *he* didn't get custody. Those reasons might still be relevant today."

"What? I don't get it. You said you want me to know my relatives."

Careful now, she told herself. Her head was about to burst. "I agree it would be good for you to know them and have some connection, but only if they're healthy people, and when they can be of help to you, not when they could drag you down. Your birth dad's troubles might still be an issue for him and Anna may have her own problems."

"You're so mean. Why are you saying that? He's part of me." Shayla's face was distorted, and Bernice knew her sensitive daughter was close to losing it, tears already rolling down her cheeks. She stepped forward and put her hand on her arm, but Shayla shrugged her off. She tried to modulate her voice, speaking as softly as she could and with compassion.

"We don't have to talk about that right now, honey. All I'm saying is that we'll have to go slow. As your parents, Dad and I need to protect you. We love you. Sorry honey, I'm not feeling well; I have to lie down. We'll discuss it later, when Dad is home." She moved away from Shayla towards her bedroom.

Seeing her mother leave, Shayla stamped her foot on the ground, then turned around and ran down the stairs, shouting: "You don't understand me at all; you don't know anything!" She slammed her bedroom door shut. The explosion of dry wood against dry wood forced Bernice to close her eyes and cover her eyes in an attempt to contain her pounding headache.

That didn't go as planned; she did understand what she had done wrong and why her daughter behaved like a ten-year-younger version. What she didn't get at all is how she herself could have misjudged the situation so badly. Was her relationship with Shayla not as solid as she thought? How could this man, this stranger who hadn't been around – and certainly never had a relationship – incite this much passion in her daughter? Was Shayla's attachment to them only superficial? Had she and Tom failed?

She lay down on the bed with a wet cloth on her forehead, trying not to think, as she observed the red light with its exploding stars behind her closed eyelids. She listened to the throb of her circulation through the veins in her head.

After about ten minutes, the light effects calmed down and a thought arose: Shayla finally demonstrated some healthy teenage rebellion. Oh, her head needed a break. She carefully opened her eyes, got up slowly, and when moving didn't intensify her headache, she went to the bathroom cabinet, took two of her migraine painkillers, and closed the heavy drapes, shutting out all light.

She wished Tom were home. She wasn't getting what she needed from him, wasn't up to dealing with her mounting problems with Shayla without him. Her stomach rebelled; she got up and just got to the bathroom in time to vomited in the bowl, until she had nothing left in her body. She laid back down on the king-sized matrimonial bed, so terribly tired all of a sudden that she could cry, and tears did seep through her closed lids onto the pillow, one by one.

CHAPTER 7

Shayla's pillow was wet with tears. Lying on her stomach, she was panting; her sinuses were completely stuffed up. She gave free reign to her grief, shoulders heaving. Her heart felt small and sore with a thrumming beat it could barely contain, as if it was going to explode and she'd die. Her thoughts were in a jumble. She didn't try to muffle her sobs and wasn't thinking about anybody else: She was alone in the world. Nobody could help her; nobody understood her.

After a while, her vigorous crying slowed down to another sound – a yelp every few seconds, like a puppy in distress – and the flow of tears stopped; she had no more left. She tried opening her eyes, but they were swollen and wanted to stay closed. Her arms and legs were ice cold. She turned around and pulled her bedspread over herself. Her mind slowed; her spirit needed a rest. She faded off into a deep sleep.

It was suppertime when Shayla woke up, disoriented. Her throat was sore and her head was about to burst. The full extent of the disaster came flooding back to her: Her mom wanted to keep her away from her relatives. She trusted Bernice and even loved her – up to now. Is this the reward she got for that trust? She worked so hard for such a long time to be good, to be respectful, and to blend in with this family

– strangers, really – and she had managed that very well. She deserved some respect and consideration. So why didn't she get it?

She remembered how hard it was to see Abby cry so much without being able to help her. She told her to forget their old mom and Uncle, and to trust their new parents. Recalling that time, she didn't remember her relief, when another adult came into their lives and finally took over from her – until now – and she realized Bernice had replaced her as Abby's protector.

But now she was 17, strong and grown up. She should be given responsibilities for her own life and she'll prove to them she was ready. A plan started shaping up. She would talk to her parents, starting with Dad; he would surely listen to her. Mom was stubborn, and she thought she knew everything, because of her job – too much of a social worker. Then Shayla's thoughts arrived at the point she always turned away from, that moment where she felt strange, when a tightness arose in her body that she couldn't place, casting a shadow of doom.

She pushed a little farther, remembering that her mom did *not* like Bernice. It had taken a long time before Shayla's memory faded of her mother's anger and of the things she had yelled at Bernice. Eventually, it all became less important and she had started calling Bernice Mom. Yes, Bernice could be unbending, but was always fair; only now Shayla didn't understand why Bernice – who said she loved her – turned against her.

She decided to stay in her room and wait till Dad got home. She wasn't hungry anyway and could eat the granola bars left over from her school lunch, if she'd get an appetite. Dad had been working late often this week; he hadn't been home for supper each day, as he used to. She would wait till Jon, Danny and Abby were in bed, and then come down to talk.

38

She turned on her laptop, checked her messages and the updates on her Facebook page, hovering the curser over the reply box at Anna's message. She restrained her impulse to click the mouse and decided to wait till after her talk with Dad, aware of some heavy feeling in her stomach that wasn't hunger. She didn't want to burn her bridges.

Shayla got up from her bed and looked in the mirror. Her face was a mess. Tears had streaked her face with black mascara and her eyes seemed as if someone had punched both eyes. She went to work fixing herself up. She needed a nice warm bath and then she'd chat with Anita. She was disgusted with everybody and didn't want to be with people – she corrected herself: not with adults. Fortunately, she had her own bathroom. Just then, her mom knocked on her door.

"Sweetheart, are you okay? Can I come in?"

"I'm okay, but you can't come in. I'm mad at you."

"Can't we talk about it?"

"I'll talk when Dad is home. I want to be alone now. Can you leave me alone, please?"

"Aren't you hungry, honey? I can bring you a plate down, if you like?"

"No, thanks. I'm not hungry. Like, I will get something myself when I want some food. When will Dad be home?"

"I'm not sure, honey. I'll tell him to see you when he gets home, okay?"

"Okay."

An hour later, smelling lovely, her skin moisturized with orange-scented body lotion, Shayla picked up her cell phone, climbed on her queen-sized sleigh bed, and punched in Anita's number. She sent a text that she needed to talk. Anita responded immediately: Wr r u, y not answer my txt b4? Shayla pushed the talk key and they were speaking.

"You'll never believe what happened. I got a message from my sister."

"Omigod, you have another sister? You never told me."

"You knew I was adopted, right? My sister, she's an adult, like, from another dad and she asked to be my friend on Facebook and I said yes. You know what? She's seeing my birth dad and she tells me he wants to see me too, and look after me and my little sister." The last words came rolling out in speed language without pause between words.

"Creepy! How can that be? Like, why not before? You already have a family now. Or do you want to live with him?"

Shayla hadn't thought that far ahead and Anita's questions made her think. "Good question. I'm not sure, I don't know. To tell you the truth, I only remember him faintly, like, he was a sad man; that's what I feel when I think of him – sad. I always felt sorry for him those few times I saw him. I don't know why. But, like, I want to know my birth father and I want to see him. Is that wrong of me?"

"No, I don't think it's wrong. But, it's like, crazy, and what about your dad that you live with; don't you like him?"

"Yes, I do; of course. He's great. I really like him; I love him. I'm waiting for him to come home and talk about it. He's so much easier to talk to than my mom. But, the other one is my biological dad; I want to have a dad like everybody else, and see what he looks like. Maybe I look like him."

"It sucks being adopted. How come you were adopted? Where was he before, do you know? And why didn't he look after you and Abby?"

40

"Crazy, but I've got no idea. He wasn't living with my mother. I remember a few visits with him at the office, at the foster home, and at my mom's funeral. He cried, like, the whole time, and then he was gone, like, he didn't even say goodbye, just disappeared, while we were eating lunch next door to where her body was. That was the last I heard from him. He was weird; I wonder what was wrong with him."

"What happened to your mother? Why did she die?"

"I think it was a car accident. I remember a whole bunch of people at the funeral. I was only ten and I had written some stories and poems for my mom in a letter. Like – embarrassing! I read the letter on the podium for everybody to hear, and then my foster mom and I put the letter and poems at her feet in the casket."

"Omigod, wasn't there a lid on it?"

"No. Like, it was awful when I saw her. She didn't even look like my mom and she had makeup on. She never wore any, and her hair was all weird. I thought maybe it was a doll, like in the wax museum. "

"Oh Shayla, that's awful. How could you stand it?"

"Yeah, and my mom's bike jacket hung on a stand next to her casket. I didn't even know she was a biker chick, like, I never had a bike ride with her. And then a whole bunch of people I didn't even know, hugged me and cried all over me. Lots of them were dressed like bikers."

"Your mom was in a biker gang?"

"I guess so, never thought of it that way. I suppose that Anna was there too, but I really didn't remember her, like, until she messaged me, just yesterday. It was all so very confusing; my social worker and my foster parent were there with us and took care of everything. Later my social worker became my adoptive mother."

"Bernice? Really? Cool; you never told me that. Did you have other brothers or sisters?"

"Yes; they were there too. I think I got two older brothers. Like, I can't really remember; they were almost adults, and came from another province with a different father. Only Abby is from the same father."

"What does your mom think about you seeing your father, I mean your first dad? Like, if she was your social worker, she would know a lot about your family."

"She's always been very good and never put them down or anything, but then, like, she was weird today, when I asked about seeing Anna and my birth dad. We got into a big fight."

"Why? What about?"

"Anna said he told her he wanted Abby and me to come and live with him. Like, my mom doesn't understand that I want a real dad. She was so mean, and I yelled at her and then I cried my eyes out." Shayla's heart started beating faster and her voice went up in pitch, accelerating.

"Wow, that's a big deal, Shayla! Scary. I can't imagine leaving my mom and and living with somebody else. Like, you don't even know him anymore."

"That's what my mom said. I don't know him. Doesn't matter; he's my birth dad."

Anita shared her own secrets. "I've never ever seen my dad. My mom left him when she was pregnant. Back then, she was living on Haida Gwaii where she was born as a band member. She left him behind and went to Vancouver, and then she moved here a year or so later. Like, he doesn't even know she was pregnant and she won't tell me who he is, and just told me he's not a good person. Maybe he was into drugs or other weird stuff. Hey, maybe that's what's wrong with your dad too."

"Haida is First Nation, right? I didn't know you're First Nation."

"Yeah, both my parents are, and I have status too. That might help me, if I ever get to post-secondary education. Where did you think I got my tan from?" Anita laughed heartily at Shayla's surprised chuckle, then she continued: "There must be a reason why he disappeared and left you two behind. I can't believe you don't even know. Did you get into foster care after your mom died?"

"Not really. I was already in a foster home when she died. I'm not really sure why. I hardly ever lived with my mom. Like, she was always gone, and never slept at our house, although she kept a bedroom, but her room was full of junk and empty suitcases. A friend of hers looked after us, Uncle Pat; he was sick most of the time. Like, I do remember my house was very dirty, that, and we had fast food all the time, like lots of pizza, or hamburgers and fries. But Uncle Pat was nice to us and we missed him for a while."

"That's so weird you never told me about this. Like a secret door opening up. Why didn't you tell me?"

While talking about the life she'd tried so hard to forget, her breathing was almost normal and her heartbeat had settled. In a much calmer voice she replied to Anita's question. "Why should I? When we're together with Ellen I always feet left out. Like, I wasn't going to tell weird things about me, so you guys could bug me some more, right?"

"We bug you? Omigod, we would never. Like, you can tell us; we're best friends. I swear I'll never bug you about your adoption, honest!"

Shayla changed the subject, thinking she'd have to see proof first. "Did you see that Eric was into Ellen at the party? Does she think he's hot? What did she tell you?"

"She's just getting to know him, because you said you think he's hot. Like, she's jealous, because Eric thinks you're hot. You know that, didn't you?"

"No, not really. To be honest, I'm not really sure what she thinks." A knot formed in her stomach when she started talking about Eric and her scalp was suddenly hot, and her hair felt prickly, like cactus spines instead of hair. Drops of sweat collected on her forehead. She walked back into the bathroom, took off her bathrobe, opened a window for cool fresh air to run over her body, placed the phone on the toilet seat on speaker. "Did he say anything to Ellen about me?" She bent over, and vigorously rubbed her scalp with her hair falling down over her face.

"You'd have to ask Ellen yourself, sweetie," echoed the voice. "You and Eric would make a better couple. Anyway, Ellen is into Jake now."

"Oh, shut up." She was cooled off, put her robe on, walked back to her room.

"You shut up. For real. You should get together at the next party; I'll help you set it up. Ellen's mom said she'd go away and let her have the house for her birthday party. Maybe you can stay overnight. Kyle promised he's coming. We'll have some fun. I got to go; my mom is calling."

"OK."

"Good luck with talking about your father with your dad; that sounds funny. No kidding, I mean it. That must be hard. Let me know how it went."

Shayla sank back on her bed. Crying and the nap had calmed her, as if her inner system had been rebooted. She had a lot to cry about lately, but was amazed that her buddy Anita asked exactly the same questions she had in the back of her mind, but hadn't admitted to

44

herself she had any. She got dressed, put on her sweats and a hoody, ready to defend her desires. Did she want to live with her birth dad? No, not like this: She definitely wanted to meet him, but first had to know a lot more about him.

She gladly took Anita's opinion that Ellen wasn't after Eric for the truth, and a new appreciation for her friends took hold. Her first real crush – could he be hers? Most of her friends had sex; it was time she got on with it. Her heartbeat accelerated, her lips curled into a smile and her eyes faded out to dream distance. She swung her arms around herself and hugged her torso tightly. That's how it should be: Someone holding her tight, cherishing her. Eric would be her chosen one, her gateway to real life and to becoming an adult. He would belong to her, and she'd belong to to him – completely.

Shayla stood at the bottom of the stairs and hesitated. Looking up, she could see part of the living room upstairs and her dad pacing from one end to the other. Although Shayla couldn't see her from where she stood, she just knew that her mom was sitting with a stiff back, being "official". They weren't talking.

She formulated the most urgent questions on her mind since her birth dad had surfaced. What did she want to know most? When she told Anita about the funeral, her whole body felt tight and she had that sick sense in her stomach, all during their conversation. She still wasn't hungry, in spite of having missed her supper.

"Oh, there you are, honey," her dad called out, noticing her at the bottom of the stairs.

"Hi, Dad." She slowly walked up, holding on to the banister for dear life, afraid her knees wouldn't hold her. Her dad walked over and hugged her briefly, then gently led her with an arm around her shoulders to the couch. "It's been an exciting day, I hear. What's up? Mom tells me you want to talk to me?"

"Yes, I want to ask you some things, but she'll have to leave first." Her head turned with a quick jerk in the direction of her mother; she glanced quickly at Bernice without making eye contact.

"But, honey, Mom and I don't keep secrets from each other and she's very much concerned about you too. I think she should hear this."

Shayla looked down at her hands, inspecting her nail polish. "We had a fight. She doesn't understand me and she always makes me feel like I'm a dumb child, who doesn't know anything. Like, I'm old enough to know some things, you know."

Her mom got up from the couch, eyes wide with genuine surprise, and started to approach her to make some sort of physical contact, but Shayla stepped back to ward off an unwanted hug from her mom, before Bernice could touch her. "Oh, sweetheart, I didn't know. I don't mean to; I apologize I made you feel that way."

Shayla shrugged her shoulders and finally looked at her with a cold stare. "Are you leaving or not?" She noticed her dad looking at her mom with pleading eyes, but he stayed silent. Her mom looked back at him, eyebrows still raised, body leaning forward, as if frozen in midair, like in a still photograph. As if suddenly touched by a magic wand, she came to life from her spell, walked down the hall to the bedrooms, and speaking over her shoulder to the living room space in general, she said: "I'll be in our bedroom, if anybody wants to talk to me."

46

CHAPTER 8

Bernice sat down on the bed in the spacious bedroom and turned on the gas fireplace, to add some comfort on the chilly April evening. She shivered, her legs were shaky; suddenly she was too tired to even lift a dress over her head. She fell back on the bed without undressing, spread her arms wide, and stared at the ceiling, her legs dangling off the end. Her thoughts ran amok circling around Shayla's rejection, completely thrown off by Shayla's preference of Tom over her as confidant.

Slowly, reason took hold of her: So be it, let Tom deal with her. At least he was useful where she couldn't go. Shayla always was more susceptible to Tom's opinions, solely by the grace of his gender, probably to do with the missing father-figure. She wondered what he was going to tell Shayla; they hadn't discussed what to say in particular, assuming she would be there as well – Bernice had all the facts. It hadn't turned out that way and she wished Tom good luck.

Her confrontation with Shayla brought back memories of those stressful events of seven years ago. She was surprised to hear he was still alive, and the thought of that man coming back into her daughter's life was just too much to bear. In that week after their mom's death, the children talked about their mom and the times when she'd occasionally drop in at Uncle's to bring presents and treats. The person they mostly talked about was Uncle Pat, seldom not their mom, and never about their dad.

As it turned out, knowing that a car accident had taken away their mom, rather than finding out she hadn't cared enough to fight for them, had been a blessing in disguise. She told Angela about it as they went through the process, back then. "Her accidental death is helping Shayla and Abby to move on from a parent's death faster than I've ever seen with any other child. I think that's because they already had given up on their mom years before her death, when Uncle started in his caregiving role."

"You might be right. Their briefest of grieving was more for the idea of a mother."

As it happened, the girls' sadness quickly changed into excitement and hope for their new life with Wanda. They soaked up the attention, like a desert absorbing rain without so much as a trace of a puddle left behind.

Bernice had discussed the circumstances with the adoption worker and shared she experienced most satisfaction from working with parents who wanted their children back and regained custody by addressing their issues. If not for those family reunions, her vocation would be bleak and hold little intrinsic reward, but this case had been different. Deeply disturbed by Nora's lack of interest in her children, Bernice confessed she let the children attach to her. Like Wanda, she felt a special bond, although she hadn't anticipated to get strongly attached to them so instantly. They quickly arrived at the only solution – adoption.

Bernice heard shouting coming from downstairs. Quickly she pulled herself together and opened her bedroom door a crack.

"Why do you always choose her side? It's not fair. I have a right to see my dad. Why won't you let me? You can't tell me what to do: You're not even my real dad!"

"Sweetheart, don't run off, listen to me…" she heard Tom pleading. Loud stomping followed. Quickly she closed her door and sat down on the love seat by the window, waiting. A few seconds later she heard the front door slamming shut. From her perch by the window she saw Shayla leaving, her coat half on, madly stamping her feet while disappearing down the garden path and around the corner at the end of their street.

She waited, unsure how to react to the rebellious behaviour of her daughter and the unusual confrontation with her dad – that was a first. Tom didn't get into conflicts with anybody, let alone with Shayla, the apple of his eye. He must be more impatient than usual. She'd hardly seen him this week; he must be overloaded at work.

After the economic slowdown, he had taken over listings from other realtors that quit. Although every family had to do more with less, Tom had been extremely diligent in ensuring his job of the provider of his family was secure. She also knew he'd always considered her job as a nice addition – good for the luxuries in life and vacations. When was their last real vacation, anyway? She couldn't remember. It was time to have another one.

She wondered why Tom wasn't coming upstairs to talk to her. She left the room and looked for him, didn't see him in the family room downstairs, but found him in his den behind his laptop. He quickly closed his laptop when Bernice entered his den. "Well, that was interesting. What happened?"

With a frown, Tom looked at Bernice and a sneer formed around his mouth. "I don't know. She seemed hell-bent on seeing this man; I lost my patience. What does she think he could do for her, anyway? From what I understand, he couldn't be bothered to show up for her childhood, so why is he all of a sudden so important to her? Can you make an educated guess?"

Having been sidelined, her time to think had helped to get some clarity and she slowly replied. "I'm not sure what's gotten into her. Maybe it's just a belated response to something we've missed. I have to admit, I'm at a loss of what she might be going through, but maybe we should be glad she is finally rebelling and trying to find her own way."

"Frankly, I'm insulted. All these years we are *it* and I'm her daddy, and now this stranger shows up and wants to take her home with him – the gall to even propose that to her. I'm pretty damn mad at both, to tell you the truth. And mad at myself for caring so much."

"Yes, I can see you're angry. Actually, I'm quite annoyed myself. Did she share anything with you?"

"No, I hardly could get a word in; she just told me a rambling story about her sister and her dad and all getting together as a family and that he had never a been given a chance to look after her, although he had wanted that very much. I said I thought we're her family and that he'd never stepped up to the plate anyway, and how could he, as an addict. I shouldn't have not let her talk me into talking without you." Now there's a discovery, but she stayed silent.

He rubbed his face with both hands, then one hand went up to touch his bald spot on top of his head, and he rubbed it vigorously, then he rubbed his neck with both hands where he felt the strain from bending long hours over his laptop. Bernice walked over to him, stood behind his chair and massaged his shoulders and neck.

"How's that feel?" she asked gently. Tom ignored her question, but didn't move away from her hands. She continued: "She and I had the same argument. I've been thinking, Tom. Maybe it's time to share more with her about her relatives. I'm not sure about the timing, as she might see it as badmouthing her natural family, the way she feels nowadays. I wonder why she's so – what shall I say – so prickly and critical. Do you think there's something else going on?"

"What could there be? She's doing well in school and in ballet. She has some best friends; When she left in a huff, she said she was going to Anita. She'll be back soon, you'll see. Luckily there's no boyfriend in the picture, as far as I know." He turned around and looked at her.

Bernice stopped massaging for a few seconds and restarted in rhythm with her sentences, slowly sharing what she knew. "I think there may be a crush involved; she told me about it the other day, but she's not sure whether its mutual. Well, yes, this is a nerve-wracking time for all girls. According to the literature, all the major milestones in life become a bigger hurdle for kids who've lost a parent early, and those who had a difficult childhood – she got two for two. I guess the old distrust of adults resurfaces at those times."

She stopped massaging his shoulders and came around in front of him and sat down on the ottoman. In spite of the massage, he looked at her with the frown still there, and with hostile eyes.

"Why do I only get to hear that now? Why didn't you tell me earlier? Isn't that important? I would've liked to know that before my talk with her."

"Don't blame me. Not my fault. I wanted to tell you, but you're always working late. Do you remember how she was in the beginning with us, so polite, but standoffish and distant? That was really tightly packaged sadness and distrust. But she has learned trust us. This time, she's trying to separate from us by rejecting us and fighting with us – mistrusting our motives."

"That's hard to take, but why now?"

"She's emotionally delayed, like most neglected kids. It'd be appropriate for an earlier age, say thirteen or so; she needs to sort out her own opinions, form an identity of her own."

"Okay, I'll buy that. But why the fuss about her dad? Am I not good enough?"

Bernice replied briskly: "Damn it, this isn't about you. She loves you, don't you get that? If she didn't, she wouldn't care what you'd think."

"Okay, that's true; sorry, I just don't like to fight. Her tone got to me. I've never had this kind of attitude from her before." He looked sheepishly at Bernice.

"Life was difficult for the girls and you can't blame them for looking for an easier way in life, once in a while. She just needs more time to get to independence in that respect. Maybe she's just curious, looking for a family connection, maybe find her eyes in him, or his body type, or what have you." She put a hand on his knee and smiled encouragingly, like a mother might.

"Bernice, you're so smart. You do have an answer for everything." She could see that her answers sounded reasonable to him: Time to bail, but she wouldn't let him off that easily. She moved the ottoman sideways, closer to him, blocking his way to the door.

"That didn't sound nice; who said that? Did Shayla say that to you? Or is that what you think?"

"Let's not go there now, Bernice. I'm not up to a debate. You're a strong person with a lot of wisdom, but sometimes keeping up with you it just exhausting, and I need a break. I'm not as strong as you."

"Can I ask you one question, Tom?"

"Okay, if it stays with one and you'll accept my answer."

"What kind of work do you do at night that can't be done during the day? I miss you here at home, especially with Shayla's belated adolescence breaking through, and her relatives tugging at her. Abby could be triggered by all this too – she's got the age. Would you be home more in the evenings, or is that too much to ask for?"

Bernice closed her eyes while leaning back, not wanting to look directly at Tom. She felt him watching her; he didn't answer. Were his eyes scanning her face, looking for signs of forgiveness, of tolerance, of sweetness, hoping to find another personality than she had? She opened her eyes and observed him, saw his arm muscles flexing, his feet underneath him, soles flat on the floor, but he couldn't leave: She was blocking his way out of the den. A few minutes went by without either one speaking. Then his cell phone rang.

"Hello, Tom here." Some female voice was on the other end; Bernice studied his face that remained completely blank. "Yes, I could get that now, if you're okay with that. I do need it as soon as possible. Yes, in half an hour. Thanks a lot. I appreciate it."

He stood up and turned to Bernice. "Sorry, I've to go to the office. To answer your question: I'm extremely busy and no, some of that work cannot wait. I might lose the sale, when I'm not quick and competitive enough in this market. Anyway, I prefer to finish my work for the day and start a new day fresh. Sorry again. We'll talk soon, I promise."

When she moved out of his way, he quickly left without a kiss or a goodbye. The day before, he had stayed downstairs to work in his den and must have slept on the family room couch, as he did not come to bed that night.

53

Bernice's migraine returned with an intensity that usually stopped her from functioning. Around 10:30 p.m. Shayla came home. She went straight to her room, but couldn't avoid her mother, standing in the doorway of her bedroom, looking pale, as if in pain. "How's things with you, sweetheart? Are you okay?"

"I'm fine. I went to Anita; she understands me. You look sick." Shayla looked fine.

"That's good. I'm very happy you have some good friends. I'm fine with talking things over when you want to, but not now; it's too late and I've got a headache. We'll talk tomorrow after supper, okay? You can ask me then everything you want to know and I'll give you an answer to all your questions. Sweet dreams, honey." She walked over to Shayla and hugged her. To her relief, Shayla hugged her back.

"Okay, Mom."

She went to bed; Tom hadn't come home yet. Bernice fell in a deep sleep on account of her migraine meds. She woke up from a dream, when she heard the garage door opening; she turned on her other side and fell right back into a deep, dream-free sleep.

CHAPTER 9

Saved by the bell. Tom went upstairs to the bathroom and splashed some aftershave on his face. No, he'd better not change shirts; that would make it too obvious. He hurried out of the house, started his Volvo station wagon and opened the garage door with the remote control. He noticed a tight band around his stomach and a flutter in his heart. His breath was shallow and quick.

His thoughts became very focused on how he acted, trying to assess what he would look like from another's viewpoint. He didn't want to make any mistakes. He didn't really know what was going to happen when he would meet Marla at the office, but anticipation of something great took over. He just knew something surprising was about to take place.

He completely banned any thoughts about what had just happened between him, Shayla, and Bernice, driving faster than he should, to arrive sooner, rather than later, before he changed his mind. At the office, the middle-aged, uniformed security man was just leaving the building, greeting him with a "Goodnight, sir, working late?"

"Yes, can't be helped, all in a day's work. Just leave the front door open, will you? I'll lock up myself." Ten minutes passed; every few minutes Tom looked at his wall clock, unable to concentrate on the numbers before him. He was supposed to do a market analysis of comparable recent sales in the area to justify the proposed asking price for a client. His company's staff parking was located at the back of the building; his office on the second floor looked out over it. He couldn't stay seated in his chair and kept getting up to have a peek outside. A car drove up. Tom looked down from his window. It was Marla.

He took his jacket off and rolled up his sleeves. It was almost May and balmy in the evening; with an adrenalin rush heating up his system, he wouldn't feel any cold anyway. He felt his armpits moisten and a faint smell of sweat hit his nose. He wished he'd kept extra clothing in his office and reminded himself to bring a few shirts next time. Just in case, he wrote it down on his notepad.

He opened his desk drawer, took out two glasses and placed them on his desk. Then he walked to the bar fridge in the corner. He kept some beverages there; he liked a cold drink of water on a hot day and was known to offer something stronger to his guests, to celebrate a sale, or soothe each other when an important sale fell through. He kept some white wine and some beer in his office, just for those occasions, and for Marla a dry Chardonnay. He handily opened the bottle with the professional, levered corkscrew in one fluid movement, just as Marla stepped into his office.

On seeing the wine glasses, Marla hesitated a second, then stepped into the space with a smile on her face, flawlessly made up, as usual. Tom approached her, put an arm around her slim shoulders and kissed her on the cheek bending down. He held his face close to her blonde, shoulder-length hair a few moments longer, softly commenting: "Marla, you smell so wonderful." Then he quickly stepped back, offering her the chair in front of his desk, and sat down on the other side.

Marla was wearing a black pencil skirt and a low-cut cowl neck sweater of a silky, turquoise material that fell smoothly around her perfect torso. "Would you like a glass? We might as well make the best of it; don't you agree?"

"Sure, why not? I see you got my kind of wine. Thanks; how thoughtful of you." She looked at him with a question on her face. Tom studied her expression, trying to gauge what she might be thinking. Was he too presumptuous already offering wine while they were still in the office?

"Yes, I remember from last time. The look on your face tells me that you want to ask me something."

"Actually, yes. Tom, we're here to work on the market analysis, are we not? I want to just be clear about what it is we're doing." Her tone was light and her face all smiles.

"Yes, of course, Marla. But, to be honest, I was hoping you would let me take you out tonight. I so enjoyed our time together and I feel you did, too, or am I wrong? I wonder what you think about me." He cast his eyes down, just like twenty years ago, when courting Bernice; she always said his shyness got her.

"Tom, I like you and I liked being out with you the last time. I think you're a great man to work for. I think your wife is a lucky lady. I'm sure she does appreciate you. Are you happily married?" Going right for the kill, she was.

"Now, right there, that's the problem. But, we won't talk about that now. Let's get this thing on the road. We'll have more time to talk, when we're done. But I'm really happy that you like me. You really are helping me out a lot with this extra work. I just want you to know that."

They worked steadily for about an hour; it wasn't that big a job. Tom poured Marla another glass, but didn't drink more himself. At one point he pulled up another chair – very close to her – so they could together compare the documents' data side by side. He could sense in his nose and mouth the faintest smell of some French perfume. He desperately wanted to kiss her. He did not, with great self-control, unsure whether she would withdraw from him, and then the mood would be spoiled.

Finally, the job was done and they left the office together. They had decided on a nice lounge downtown connected to one of the higher end hotels, but Tom didn't tell her he picked it as none of his acquaintances would watch a game there or take the wife for a drink. Tom locked the office door, then gallantly held her elbow, afraid she might trip on her high heels while walking down the stairs. He locked up the building and led Marla to his vehicle.

When she turned her face towards him, she maintained eye contact – he thought she was seeking his approval – while her golden hair softly bounced around her shoulders. Marla was a foot shorter than he; walking beside her, he stretched out to his full length. She chatted incessantly. Not a watcher of the type of shows she was referring to in her stories, Tom didn't know what she was talking about. He wasn't asking any questions and stayed at the receiving end of the conversation.

On entering the lounge, he put an arm around her shoulders and pulled her closer to him. She didn't draw back and seemed to like his gesture. They chose a booth in a rather sparsely lit corner, removed from the few guests, still at the hotel bar at this late hour. Tom ordered a bottle of local Chardonnay without asking Marla. When she raised her eyebrows, he commented: "Don't worry; I'll make sure that you get home okay." She smiled.

He just watched her, drinking in her image, every facial asset, her feminine mannerisms, her perfect hair, her peachy skin, manicured hands and nails: She was a dream. He wondered whether young women knew how beautiful they were. He poured more wine – she didn't object this time. After the second glass – really her fourth, counting the drinks at the office – Marla started to lean into him, touch him on the arm, then touched his hand a few minutes later, and then, finally, put her hand on his knee, while chatting and laughing loudly about his corny jokes.

Tom ordered another bottle. When it arrived with the waiter, he took the bottle from the cooler and poured Marla another glass, and a short while later, unable to stop himself, he had another glass as well, while Marla slowed down and skipped a round. She was leaning into him with her whole upper body, so that the kiss was unavoidable. He stroked her hair and rolled a few strands on his finger and gently pulled her face towards him. They kissed again and again.

Marla's eyes were sparkling and her lips were very red; she had a natural, rosy glow on her cheeks. Tom was making the girl dance to his tune, like the pied piper. How delicious. Their hands started traveling, exploring other areas. Tom felt her right hand moving towards his crotch while she breathed heavily into his neck, her hair in his face.

His erection was immediate. Startled, he grabbed her hand, pulled her even closer and whispered in her ear: "I couldn't stop thinking about you after our kiss last week; I want you so badly." His left hand hesitantly slid around her back and cupped her soft and smallish breast over her top for just a second. The booth wasn't comfortable anymore – this wasn't him. He released her breast and her hand and pulled away, then drew his arm around her shoulders and studied Marla's face, when he made his proposition: "Marla, don't take this the wrong way, but what would you say about getting us a room, here in the hotel, to talk some more in private, if you're up to it. I'll let you have the room and take a cab in the morning. We both had too much to drink to be driving home safely."

He sounded like a cliché in a cheap novel, but that's all he knew to say; it was his first time and he hadn't expected this speedy progress. With Bernice, it had taken weeks before he got this far in their courting. When she replied, her words were slurred.

"A wonderful idea, and so considerate of you. Yes, I'm ready." He put his arms around her waist, bent over her and tried to pull her gently out of the booth. She planted a full kiss on his right eye before she rose to her feet. "I am not much of a drinker," she admitted.

They left the lounge, Marla walking unsteadily on her stilettos with Tom's arm around her waist, ready to catch her in case she tripped. The receptionist was discreet and quick, not giving them time for changing their minds. On the fifth floor they let themselves into a room and fell down on the king-sized bed and continued from where they'd left off in the booth. Their lovemaking was all he had imagined, fuelled by a week of longing and plenty of wine.

———

Tom startled awake, wondering where he was for a second, until he saw Marla in the faint glow from the street lights through the open curtains. He looked at his watch: One o'clock in the morning. Marla was snoring lightly, her head resting on her pillow. He watched her for several minutes, enjoying her beautiful, voluptuous body sprawled out over the bed. She was lying on her back, like a painting of a Dutch master; his eyes followed her lines from her legs all the way up to her face – a perfect picture. As his eyes lingered, he inhaled deeply, the air inflating his chest enhancing his sense of well-being. Then he slowly exhaled. What more to be desired than to have been the object of this woman's desire and admiration?

He recalled this sense of well-being from many years earlier – just out of high school – but now he had money to burn and the wisdom of experience, a wonderful time of life and he deserved it. It dawned on him that he should leave, if he wanted to do things right and not spoil it. He got up and gently pulled the light cover from the foot of the bed over Marla, careful not to wake her. He found a note pad in the desk and wrote her a note: Thanks so much for a wonderful evening. You are beautiful. See you soon. He got dressed, then gently closed the door behind him and made his way to his car, now completely sober.

On arrival at his nice Craftsman-style home under as dark sky, dawn still hours away, he approached his driveway slowly and turned off the car's headlights. He snuck into his home like a vampire making his way into his coffin in the crypt. He took off his jacket, folded it neatly and laid it on the floor. He fell down on the couch while pulling a throw from the backrest over himself, and fell into a deep sleep. He must have been dreaming about his adventure, as a smile appeared on his face.

What seemed only a few minutes later, Jonathan was jumping on him. "Dad, Dad, wake up. Mom tells you it's time to get up, or you'll be late for work. Will you be at my practice? Mom says she can't do it today."

"What? I'm up. Get off me, will you, and calm down. You're getting too heavy to jump on me. You'll give me a hernia. Where's your practice today?" Tom sat up and put his feet on the floor, his head heavy and his brain foggy.

"It's at the middle school sports fields, at six. Will you be there? Can you, please, please?"

"Sure, I'll make time for it; you're my soccer hero, of course I'll come. Now get ready for school. Hurry up, off you go." He gave his son a gentle rub on his head with his knuckles and Jon ran off, up the stairs, towards the kitchen. The sound of children chatting and of early morning family traffic reached Tom; he put on his clothes and slowly took the stairs, tread by tread, bracing himself for the onslaught of four children and a wife.

"Good morning, everybody." Tom stroked Daniel's head and in the next second ruffled up his son's long hair with both hands. He hated his son's long locks. Daniel pulled his head away.

"Hi, Dad."

"How are my girls?"

"Okay."

"Fine."

Bernice's question hit Tom square in the brain. "Where were you all night?"

"I wasn't gone. I slept downstairs after I came home late; I'm not sure what time. I didn't want to wake you. But I did finish what I set out to do last night." If he were a cat, he would purr.

"I wished you'd at least call me. I worry about you. I haven't seen a lot of you lately." She was beginning to sound like a nagging wife, Tom thought.

"Sorry, I'll try to think of it, but when it gets that late, I would just wake you up. Well, today I have some time. What do you say, want to go out for dinner later tonight, just us? I'm sure the kids will be all right with Shayla; we can pay her for babysitting."

"No, silly; you're supposed to go to the soccer practice with Jon, unless you want to go after practice. He just asked you; didn't you hear?"

"Yes, I did, but why can't you do it?"

"We agreed that's your job. Besides, I have a late meeting I couldn't avoid. You'll have to pick up Jonathan from the house and take him to practice."

"Bummer." He didn't know exactly why he exasperated his disappointment, but realized it in the next moment.

Always accommodating, Bernice reacted. "How about we go for dinner tomorrow instead? It's my flex day. I could run errands during the day and do some house cleaning before the weekend. I can be ready when you arrive home from work. A day off from work and an evening out with you would make it a perfect day. Shayla has ballet practice tomorrow after school, but she'll be finished by six. What do you say, dinner at seven thirty?"

"That sounds great." What else could he say? "I had better enter Jon's soccer practice on my calendar, before I forget again. If you'd take my Saturday shift with Jon, that would be great, thanks. People always want to view homes on the weekend." He almost believed this excuse himself.

Bernice tacitly responded. "Okay, I'll trade with you and take him to his game on Saturday; that'll free you up, but you're skipping out on practices too often."

Tom saw she didn't like the changes. "Sorry Bernic; I'll make up for it with a nice dinner." He took his smart phone out of his pocket and punched some keys. "What do you pay Shayla per hour nowadays?"

"I give her six dollars per hour. Shayla, would you like to baby-sit tomorrow?"

Shayla did not bite immediately to this generous offer, weighing her answer while both her parents were looking at her. "How long are you out for? I had planned to meet with Anita and Ellen later that night and maybe stay overnight, if her mom says it's okay."

Tom left it up to Bernice to sort that out. "We'll have to talk about that overnight later, honey. Your dad and I won't stay out that long; we'll be back by nine at the latest, right Tom?"

"Yes, sure. Where do you want to eat? I'll make reservations. How about trying out that fancy place you were talking about the other day, by the harbour?"

"La Bouche?"

"Yeah, that one." It was settled; he was going to be free on Saturday.

CHAPTER 10

At the end of her ballet lesson, Shayla massaged her sore calf muscles with her right hand, while hanging on with her left hand to the bar attached to the wall; she had enjoyed the practice today. Ballet class was the only place where she knew what she was doing. Virginia Gambia had just dismissed the group of teen ballerinas when the dark haired woman in her forties walked from her centre position in front of the class towards her. Shayla admired her as an excellent instructor and a gentle mentor, and very pleased that Virginia had taken a shine to her.

"How are things with you, Shayla? You seemed a bit distracted today, or am I wrong about that?" She looked at Shayla with a smile on her face and inquisitive eyes.

"Eh, maybe, I'm not sure. I liked the lesson today. Those jumps are great, but I feel a little sore now."

"Yeah, good work today. Well, maybe I'm wrong, but let me know if I can help you with anything. I want you to know you've got talent and I would hate to see you lose interest in ballet when other things in your life happen. You have the potential to go far, if you stick to it. Are you having any difficulties at home or with your friends? Not that I want to pry, just so you know you can always talk to me, Shayla."

"Thanks Missus G. Me and my friends are good. But, now that you mention it, I did have a fight with my dad, and I hate fighting with him. Like, he is usually on my side. I don't want to talk about it. I'll tell you, if I can't work it out myself. Thanks for asking anyway. Have a good weekend, Mrs. G. See you next week."

"Have a great weekend, Shayla." Shayla walk out of the studio, feeling her teacher's eyes burning into her back. She had to admit it: Mrs. G's instincts were always right on the mark. Maybe she'd talk to her about Eric; it couldn't hurt having a neutral adult on her side besides her over-protective parents.

In the dressing room, Shayla's cell beeped – a text from Anita: R u cming at Ellen's house + stay ovrngt? She replied: Dn't knw yet, wll txt u. She hadn't talked about the overnight yet with her mom, afraid for her answer, and on top of that, she still needed to talk about the email from Anna and meeting their birth dad. When would it be a good time for that? Never!

Her parents were going out and her mom was probably waiting for her already outside. Her parents acted like they'd always been adults and her mom surely had never been as insecure as she was about Eric, or she'd have shown more understanding. She walked to the exit and saw her mom's car parked at the curb. She straightened her back, took a deep breath while walking up to the vehicle's passenger side, and opened the door.

"Hi honey, get in. How was class?"

"Okay. Missus G is nice. My calves are a bit sore; she had us doing lots of jumps. Where are you and Dad going tonight?"

In a hurry, Bernice pulled into traffic, careful to avoid other parents and their daughters also leaving from the curb. "Your dad made reservations for La Bouche. I haven't been there before. It'll be great to have some time to ourselves; it's been a while. So Shayla, how are you doing? Do you want to talk to me now about the email from your sister?"

"Omigod, Mom, do we have to?"

"We've got to some time, might as well do it now. I understand that your dad didn't get to explain why we're hesitating about your getting acquainted with Gabriel and Anna. You seem a little sensitive lately. Is anything wrong that I should know about?"

Shayla shrugged. "I'm fine and I don't want to talk about it now. I was very excited at first and would like to meet them both, Anna and him, like, maybe not right away. I already went over it with Anita and she had some good questions. Can we not talk about it anymore, please?" Shayla looked at her mom with pleading eyes, but her mom quickly glanced away.

"Maybe later, on the weekend then?"

"Yeah, that's way better. There's a lot going on for me, like, with graduation and Eric and all. I'm not sure that he's going to ask me for the dance. Ellen asked me to come to her house later tonight; we're having a girls' night, the three of us. Can I go when you and Dad are back from your dinner, please?" She anxiously studied her mother's face, afraid of what she might say.

Her mom was quiet for a few seconds before answering, her brow raised, then turned to her. Their eyes met and held for a few seconds, then she looked again at the road ahead of her and slowly answered. "I know your friends are important to you, Shayla. I'll only agree to your overnight stay, on the condition that you agree to have that talk

67

with me on Sunday. I'd really like to tell you more about your relatives, and why I hesitated to rekindle those ties. Do you agree? I know it's an emotional issue, but you're much too old to just throw a tantrum and run away from the truth. It's been seven years since you last saw them; you were really young and didn't know what was going on."

Shayla's anger rose again, she was about to burst out, when she saw her predicament: Getting angry would get her mom to dig in and leaving for Ellen's would be escalating the fight; she wouldn't meet Eric. She let out a deep sigh, took another deep breath and slowly let the air escape.

"Are you okay, honey?" her mother asked.

"Yes, I'm okay. That's just blackmail, Mom. How fair is that?"

"Sweetheart, that's called negotiation and is completely fair. You want something and I want something, so we trade off. Adults do that. No use complaining about it, honey."

"Then I don't want to be an adult."

"Sure you do. I don't just want to lay down the law anymore, because you're an adult, and because I think it will be good for you to hear the whole story, even if it's hard. Do we have a deal?" They drove along in silence for a few minutes; her mom used to do overwhelm her with more reasons, but seeing no other out, she replied.

"Okay, I agree. But don't try to convince me, okay? Or run after me. It's hard for me. Yes, I'm sensitive, I admit it. I always thought that my birth dad didn't love me; maybe I was wrong. Is that so bad to want your parents to love you?"

Her mom pulled over abruptly and with the motor running, turned to her, tears in her eyes and with a shaky voice said: "Of course not, honey. That's what we expect of our parents and they do love their children, even when not together. I'm sure that your birth dad does love you too. And we do too, Tom and me. Many people love you: Your sisters and brothers, grandma and granddad, and your aunties and uncles as well, and your friends. Don't you ever forget that."

"Jeez, mom, I didn't want to upset you," she said quietly. Her mom hugged her briefly and let her go again, then looked in the rear view mirror and pulled onto the road.

"That's okay, honey, I'm not upset. I'm just sad that you might think someone as important as your biological father didn't love you. I want you to feel good about yourself, because you're a wonderful young lady. My hope for you is to love yourself and let the beautiful, accomplished and kind adult who's already inside you come to life."

Hearing it put that way, Shayla realized she had put too much weight on the unknown opinion of a man she barely knew once – long time ago. The people that mattered were right here in front of her. "Okay. I'm doing my best here, Mom, but please, don't social-work me."

"Your best; that's all anybody can do. We're home. Okay, so we'll talk on Sunday then?"

"Okay. Love you, mom."

"Love you, too." They briefly hugged again, before both went into the house to get on with their plans.

Later that night, Shayla rang the door bell at Ellen's. The house was a mid-sized two-storey, split-level entry home – a rectangular box with a front door in the middle. Shayla liked how Ellen's mom had sponge-painted the main living space in an artsy pattern with a golden-brown colour, turning the bland home into quite the funky place with strong colours and a Mexican flavour. Ellen's older brother was away at college and Ellen was the only one left at home. Ellen's friends all liked to hang out at her place, not in the least because her mom was fun and sometimes joined them in a drink. She used to say: "Kids will be kids," so she didn't see a problem with Ellen's friends having a few drinks at her home, and then she'd drive them all home afterwards.

Ellen liked to make fun of her mom's story of the immigrant from Croatia and how she'd learned to drink with sensibility at no special age. As a small child she got a small sip of wine diluted with water in a tiny glass on special occasions, just to include her in the special event. That's how Ellen learned to drink too: By the time adolescence rolled around, she enjoyed a glass together with the other members of the family, just like in Croatia. Shayla wasn't judging, but saw that the Croatian method wasn't quite translating for Ellen, often drunk at parties and she suspected popular because of her easy access to alcohol.

Ellen opened the front door. Her face was a feature of artistic skill with dark blue eye shadow with black eyeliner and dark purple, almost-black lipstick. She wore a black T-shirt with horizontal cuts, revealing the tops of her breasts and her partially bare shoulders voluptuously filling her top. Compared to that outfit, Shayla was underdressed, less beautiful, and less confident in her okay-but-not-ravishing clothes, allegedly just going to Ellen's for an overnight with the girls – not to a party.

"Hi, you made it. Come in. Guess who's here?"

"I know who's here. Have you been drinking already, or what? You mean Eric, don't you?"

"Yeah, and Kyle and Jake. My mom and her guy are not coming back until after two; closing time, they said."

"Omigod, we're going to party! Can I borrow some of your make-up?"

"Sure, no problem."

They ran up the six treads towards Ellen's upstairs living room where Ellen dug out the makeup bag from her purse. Anita, her new boyfriend Kyle, and Jake – interested in Ellen – were hanging out on the couch and the chairs in varying states of elation, and of course, Eric, who was seated on the floor. The boys were having a beer. "Hi, Shayla."

She disappeared into the bathroom and put make-up on. When she came back to the room, Ellen asked if she wanted a vodka cooler.

"Cool! What do you have, peach or berry?"

"I got these low calorie Blackfly berry coolers, want to try?"

"Sure." Ingesting less calories was always a good thing for a ballet dancer.

"Here you are," Ellen said, handing her the cooler. "There's more in the fridge, help yourself." Ellen sat down on the couch beside Jake, eagerly reclaiming his attention.

Looking around the room, she wasn't sure where to sit. The others were a few drinks ahead of her and tried to talk over the loud music, their words slurred in their shouting.

"Hey, Shayla, sit with me?" Shayla felt better instantly: Eric actually talked to her. Her face got warm, and sweat prickled in her hairline. She wanted to answer, go to him, but still hesitated. "Come on, don't be shy," he called. "Who else would you talk to?"

Indeed. She saw Ellen in a deep smooch with Jake, and Anita didn't have time to turn her face to Shayla to update her on the latest gossip, deeply involved in trying to slow Kyle down in his attempts to get her to take her top off. Shayla slid down on the floor beside Eric, trying to be elegant in her wide pants. "How's things?"

"Fine."

He pulled her towards him with one arm around her shoulders and planted a kiss on the top of her head, then let his arm drop right away. "Hi, I'm glad you came. I was getting pretty bored with the company. If Ellen hadn't told me you would come for sure, I'd have left by now."

Eric had dark shoulder-length hair, about the same tint and length as hers, but without the blond highlights. He always wore it in a ponytail when playing basketball; Shayla and her friends sometimes watched the games. Eric was quite skinny and not that muscular, but his shoulders were broad, his teeth were immaculate, and Shayla had noticed he jumped higher than any of his teammates. He was a year older than Jake and Kyle and was graduating this year with the rest of his friends at another school.

"Oh, I had to baby-sit; my parents were out." She mustered all her courage and added: "I'm happy you waited. I wanted to talk to you, like, for a long time, but it never was the right time."

"Well, now it is. What would you like to talk about?"

"Like, where did you live before?"

"I'm from Toronto, but my dad got transferred here. I had to redo a year due to the move. You from here?"

They chatted for a while, until Eric took a bag of tobacco out of his pocket and a package of paper and started rolling a cigarette, then produced a small container from another pocket and poured some pot into the cigarette, finished rolling it, licked the paper and turned a nice little point at one end with his index finger and thumb. He popped the whole thing in his mouth for a second to dampen it, and lit it. He took a deep drag, held the smoke inside his lungs for a few seconds and then released it, offering the puny-looking thing to Shayla. "You smoke?" he asked with a pinched voice, trying to hold the smoke in.

She shook her head, keeping eye contact. He exhaled, releasing the blue cloud.

"Why not?" His question was direct, in a tone that was neutral, so she answered honestly.

"I don't know; I just don't like smoking. Doesn't it interfere with your basketball?"

"Actually, no. It makes me concentrate better and calms me down. I get nervous before a game and a joint works much better for me than drinking – that really slows me down. I don't care much for drinking. Not that I never drink, but I don't like to get drunk. It cramps my style," he laughed heartily.

Shayla thought he looked so very hot when he smiled and all his white teeth sparkled at her. He took another deep drag and then handed the joint to Jake, sitting closest. After a while, she asked about his parents. Eric told her his parents were still together and he was their only child.

In turn, Shayla told him about her adoption, her birth father wanting to see her, her adoptive mother having concerns about that, and her sadness about the fight with her dad, who always was on her side, but not this time. Unable to stop herself from divulging her daily worries to him, it all spilled out, because he actually listened. They were getting to know each other.

"Want to get some fresh air?" Eric got up and stretched his long legs, offering a hand up to Shayla.

"Sure," she replied and grabbed his hand, happy for the opportunity to move. She didn't like sitting there with her friends getting all heavily into making out. She felt Eric's arm around her again. They walked out of the living room – he much taller than she – down the stairs and out the back door.

From the narrow strip of lawn by the back door, the yard rose straight up to the next level, each of the three levels extensively landscaped with xeriscaping plants – only visible when the moon occasionally peeped from behind the cloud cover and slid over the garden like a lighthouse beam. They climbed the stairs of sturdy timbers to the top level, granting them a valley view – if they had looked – and sat down side by side on the largest landscape rock.

Eric leaned over slowly and kissed her once softly on her mouth. He smelled of tobacco and Axis body spray. She leaned into him and softened against him, her head on his shoulder. They sat in silence for a few minutes. He kissed her again, longer and with more passion. She didn't resist and when he let her go, she wished for it to have lasted longer.

"I like you, Shayla." He pulled out his smoking gear, rolled another joint and offered her the first drag. "Try it, you'll like it." She accepted and tried a drag, coughing hard when the harsh smoke hit her trachea, tearing up. "You'll get used to it. Next time I'll bring my vaporizer; the smoke is softer, easy to take."

She took another drag. This time she managed to carefully suck in some smoke without turning her windpipe inside out. Together they finished off the doobie. They sat quietly, Eric's arm around her, and for the first time they admired the landscape unfolding in front of them. The white spotlight of the moon overpowered the quick-retreating clouds and lit up the dark-blue sky over the lake and the town, with the snow-topped mountains in the distance.

"It's going to be a clear night," Eric knew. He let go of her shoulders and grabbed her hand, holding it firmly with both hands in his lap, sitting close beside her.

"It's beautiful," Shayla sighs.

"Yes, gorgeous," Eric answered, not looking at the moonscape. "Can I ask you something?"

"Sure, go ahead."

"Do you like me? I've liked you from the first time I saw you. You're hot and beautiful. You want to get together, like, be my girlfriend?" His voice was hurried now, quite breathless, as if he had just run up to the top of the yard.

Without missing a beat, she answered. "Yes." Then giggled.

"Really? You mean it?" With a big grin on his face he squeezed her hand, too tightly.

"Yeah. I think you're hot too, and cute; I like you. But you're hurting my hand." He let her hand go. "I was hoping you'd ask me for your grad dance, or you do you want to come to my mine?" Her own boldness startled her.

Eric didn't answer, but pulled her towards him while falling back; he slid off the big rock, pulling her with him. Both ended up on their backs facing the sky. He turned toward her leaning on an elbow, and looked at her face. Then he finally replied, solemnly. "Shayla Harrison, I would very much like to be your date for the grad." Then they kissed; this time Shayla kissed back passionately.

"Shayla, Eric, where are you?" It was Ellen, calling by the back door.

"Here, up on the hill," Shayla called out, while both she and Eric got up, and shook out their clothes to get rid of clingy bits of twigs and dirt. They slowly walked back down the landscape ties, hand in hand, towards the back door.

Ellen spoke with a thick voice, as if she had a swallowed a bee who stung her mouth on the way in, and with much dragging out of her s-consonants: "Hey you guysss, are you tired of uss, or found ssomething better to do?" she asked, laughing loudly.

Indignant, Shayla rejected the accusation. "No, we just wanted to talk. What's up?"

"Nothing much. Come insside."

They all returned to the living room where the music was still loud and the others were dancing. The party continued past one, with much laughter and joking back and forth between the friends, until Anita pointed out, "Hey Ellen, your mom will be home soon. Let's clean up this mess." Anita got everybody in on the act and soon the living room looked like nothing had been going on.

Shayla only had two coolers herself, but saw that Ellen was wasted; Anita – able to hold her liquor well through years of practice – was fine. Eric with two beers was sober enough to drive; she asked about the pot and could he drive stoned, he replied he'd be fine; he even offered to drive Jake and Kyle home, who seemed quite wasted and didn't live in the neighbourhood. The guys said goodbye and left shortly before 2 a.m. with boisterous comments, kisses and hugs.

Ellen had the large bedroom in the basement, its size the equivalence of the master bedroom upstairs. A large king-size bed took up about two thirds of the space; it even had its own gas fireplace. It was a nice sanctuary and Ellen's friends often stayed the night. They tumbled into bed, too excited to sleep.

Within minutes, Ellen's mom came home. Ellen instructed them: "Shhh. I don't want to talk to her. Pretend to be asleep." Ellen's mom moved down the stairs towards the room, peeked into the room and when she didn't get any reply to her whispered "goodnight girls" spoken in her thick accent, she softly drew the door shut. Shayla heard her footfalls going up the stairs.Anita was the first to ask. "Did you do it tonight?"

"No! Of course not, and anyway, it's none of your business. But we kissed; he's nice. He said he'll come to my grad." She was feeling very hot suddenly.

"Shut up!" Ellen said, looking at Shayla, "For real?"

"You shut up and don't pretend that you, like, came out there in the yard to call us, because you were worried about me," Shayla replied, somewhat embarrassed. "You were just nosy."

Ellen didn't deny it. "I'm hungry, you?" She opened the big bag of chips she had brought from upstairs and her friends dug in, chomping away at the salty treats. The girls chatted easily in the dark about their boyfriends, their fears, and their desires as only girls could.

Shayla knew already she was the only one of the three who still never had gone 'all the way' and her more experienced friends got a bag full of suggestions for her. "Make sure you get the pill, no, best ever is the shot: You don't want to get pregnant," Anita stated. With an abortion behind her she was the most experienced.

"Sometimes my mom stays away overnight; want to come and stay over again? Like, we get Eric to come too, and you guys can, like, do it then and not somewhere cheap, like on the back seat of car, or at a bush party, right?"

Anita commented: "Oh Ellen, you're one to talk; isn't that where you did it first, the car backseat?" Shayla remembered Anita's story and wondered why she was criticizing Ellen, when she had the same deal.

"So what? Shayla is too classy for that, and like, I want to help her."

"Thanks Ellen, so nice of you. I want to catch up to your guys, honestly – I feel like such a loser – but I've got a lot on my plate right now, like, with my birth family and stuff – I feel, like, I can't trust anybody – and I have to get my credits for grad and all. Like, I'm falling behind on my credits."

Anita interrupted. "What about trusting us?"

"I don't mean you guys, you're my friends, really the only people that I can trust. But, like, what will my parents do, if I want to be with my birth family? They're going to be mad at me; like, maybe they'll make me leave the house after graduation."

"What do you care, you're almost an adult." said Ellen, clearly sobering up.

"They've been good to me, you know. Like, I do care about them. I care about Eric too, he's so sweet, not at all what I thought about him at first. I just don't know; it's too much."

Although she couldn't see their faces, Shayla just knew that her friends were rolling their eyes, right about then. They had been over this a few times with her, and they didn't quite understand what the big deal was: Get on with it already, but they stayed quiet.

After a while, Anita asked: "Would your mom want you to go on the pill?"

"I don't know. Probably. She wouldn't want anybody to have a baby who's not ready. More work for her, huh? Right, that would have been my birth mom — having babies and not looking after them. Like, I would never do that. It's just too hard on the kids. I know!"

"Have you talked to her about your birth dad and your sister yet?"

"No, I'm scared to hear the whole story. I'm sure my mom is going to tell me all the bad things; she told me she wants to tell me more. Like, maybe I don't want to hear it, right? It's easier to only know my birth mom just died and my birth dad was gone, right? In a way, I wished he never had showed up; like, it makes everything so complicated. She allowed me to stay with you guys tonight, only if I promised that we'd have a talk tomorrow about what happened, like, with my birth parents before my adoption."

"Wow, smart move. My mom doesn't ask much of me," Ellen muttered. "She's still pissed off about my dad leaving her after they escaped from a war in Croatia."

Ellen seldom talked about her parents, so Anita asked: "He's Croatian too then? What war? Were you born here?"

"Yes, I was born there, but I don't want to talk about that. Shayla, did your mom say anything about your real dad?"

"Well, he's not my real dad; that would be my adopted dad of course. He's just my birth father, gave me his genes."

"Sure, sorry, you know what I mean," offered Ellen.

"She thinks my birth dad loves me, but how can I believe that? Like, he didn't even try to get me and Abby, and only visited us one time after my mom died, and then he disappeared. We must have scared him," she snorted, but wanted to cry.

"That sucks. But on the other hand, like, you don't know what went on, Shayla. Don't worry; you'll be okay with your mom." Anita was the wisest.

Ellen chimed in: "Oh, he's probably just another jerk, like most guys. I'm never going to tie myself down with a guy. They end up cheating on you anyway, right? Or otherwise, like, I just might cheat on him!" She laughed, a bitter sound. Anita and Shayla stayed silent.

"Shit. If you really have to know: my dad left when I was about twelve, and he started a new family; I haven't seen him since."

Shayla knew Ellen was still missing him, or she wouldn't be acting tough. The conversation slowly faded out, like a soft summer rain tapering off to just a few drops, and then nothing. When Ellen started snoring softly, Shayla turned on her side and slid into a deep sleep.

CHAPTER 11

Bernice shivered when the sun disappeared behind an occasional cloud and the breeze hit her bare skin; the wind still had a bit of a bite. Pulling the hoodie over her shoulders easily accommodated the fleeting seconds of cooler air. As the sun reappeared, the rays instantly warmed up the puff of air, like the touch of a cat's paw, and she closed her eyes, fully enjoying its unearthly tenderness. For June, it should have been warmer; nevertheless, it was lovely outside, not too warm, not too cold – a real Goldilocks moment.

The blossoming Russian olive trees that lined the creek by the water treatment plant, one street over, engulfed the entire block from their fragrant, soft-sweet yellow blooms – hardly visible on the gray foliage, but overwhelmingly present. Bernice's street ended in a cul-de-sac with a landscaped bed in its centre, surrounded by fancy brick pavers, right at the end of her driveway.

Just that morning, the city department had sent a two-person crew to tidy up the wild rose bushes, the low growing junipers, and the small Russian olive tree. As the men blew the dead leaves from the fall on a heap with a noisy gas-powered blower, the noise blew the cobwebs out of Bernice's head. Within half an hour, the bushes were also trimmed and the sprinklers fixed; the duo left, taking the brown winter refuse with them, leaving behind a perfectly groomed circle.

The wind tugged at the canvas privacy screen she'd just returned to the deck railing. Putting it up and taking it down again in the fall signified the start of a new season. As she wove the multi-metres-long canvas cloth through the bars of the railing, she recalled her childhood's kindergarten art work, kept by her mom in the attic in a box with her school projects. She wondered whether Kindergarten teachers still taught that sort of thing of weaving colourful glossy paper strips with a long flat aluminum needle through the paper mat.

Invisible behind the screen, she stretched out on her deck chair, like on a cruise ship, the sun warming her bare legs, shoulders and face, grateful for being alone at this moment, alone, no demands on her time. The young children down below rode their bikes calling each other, unaware of her presence. Later in the day, older boys would shoot hoops around the basketball stand that one of her neighbours had dragged towards the centre one year in the spring, where it sat ever since.

Bernice waited for Shayla to return from her overnight at Ellen's. She worried about what to say, fearing her girl may run, if she lost her cool like last time. She must take care to moderate her tone and think before speaking. She was leaning towards allowing Shayla email contact with Anna and delaying face-to face visits. She heard someone's steps crunching on the gravel of the drive and peeked through a gap in the canvas. Yes, it was Shayla, looking pretty happy, at first glance. Bernice got up and showed herself, and called out, "I'm up here, sweetheart."

Shayla looked up. "Hi, Mom." The front door opened and she walked up the stairs. Bernice decided to have the conversation inside, in case somebody ended up shouting. Dirty laundry must be hidden from public view, her Dutch-born mother used to say; only perfectly clean, bleached and blued laundry hung on her clothesline.

Bernice met Shayla in the upstairs living room and sat down across from her. Shayla sat with her feet steady on the floor, arms beside her and hands folded in her lap, head upright, steady gaze – good signs. She eloquently put her case before Bernice, her wishes to reconnect with her birth family, to email her sister, and her hope that she'd be allowed to see her birth father, at long last.

When Bernice was going to interrupt, she started speaking quicker, not allowing her mom to interrupt. "Mom, I just want to see what he looks like, if we have the same eyes, or maybe he likes dancing too. Like, maybe he's a musical talent, like Abby. Not knowing where you come from is so strange. It's, like, you're not born, but just fell to earth, right?"

Bernice had heard similar reasoning from other children in search of bio relatives; hearing it from her daughter startled her. "Of course you do, honey." Shayla put up her hand.

"I'm not finished, Mom. Even if he's no good and still has addictions, we'd know that soon enough, right? You would know, right? Like, I didn't mean to say that I want to leave my home and live with him. No way. That would be crazy; I couldn't bear leaving you and Abby, and Dad and the boys." She kept her eyes on Bernice while speaking, head held high – anxious, but defiant.

Bernice reached out and touched her daughter's knee. "Shayla, sweetheart, it's really okay to send Anna an email, I just wanted to talk about it with you. Last time we talked, you said that you were all excited to go and live with him, honey. That really hurt us, especially your dad. Gabriel – let's call him by his first name – couldn't stay in touch to let us know at the very least that he was still alive. With that little concern for his girls shown for that long, your dad and I think he cannot just walk in and take our girls now. We feel protective of you both. He has to prove he'll be a good influence. You understand that, don't you?"

She heard herself pleading, but failed to express her love, as planned. She stopped herself from talking. She wanted to get closer and got off the couch, took a step toward Shayla, then changed her mind and stood still, near her and ready to touch and console her when needed.

"Yes, Mom, I believe that's true, and I apologize for saying that. I just got carried away. It's sort of like, really exciting that I'll have someone I look like, with my hair or my teeth."

"Yeah, I heard that from a lot of foster children."

"With Anna I want to talk about my mom, because she's older and knows much more. I loved my mom, I mean my birth mom. I always missed her. Back then, I remember that I thought she was cool and very strong, a bit scary, but she was always nice to me and Abby. Right now, I've got so many questions. Like, we just never saw her much that I can remember, right?"

Seeing an opportunity Bernice jumped in. "You know why that was, honey, don't you?"

Shayla looked at her mother with scrunched up brow and pressing her lips. "She was busy?"

"Sweetheart, it's time to be frank with you, but, please, I don't want you to pass on to Abby what I'm going to tell you; she doesn't need to know yet."

"Okay, I won't tell Abby. Right. You can tell her when you think it' time. We're cool." She moved up close to the very edge of the couch where her mom stood, next to her, almost touching her.

She sat down next to Shayla. "Thanks, sweetheart; I appreciate your mature attitude. First off, your mother did what she thought was the right thing for you and Abby by *not* living with you two. Her life was not suitable to having children around and that life would harm you and really was unable to look after you, like your older brothers and sisters – others raised them as well – and I give her credit for recognizing that." She wasn't touching her.

"I hardly remembered my brothers." Shayla's face was open, curiosity in her eyes, and Bernice felt confident, proceeding her disclosure maintaining eye contact.

"Uncle Tim was paid to look after you both. He had a severe alcohol habit and a heart condition and must've been most of the time quite drunk, or sick. When the social workers arrived, the linens on your bed were gray from dirt, and Abby's bed had blood on the sheets; we don't know from what. You guys only ate pizzas and fast food, hamburgers and fries being the best of it."

Shayla's face lit up and pride sounded in her voice when she said: "Yes, I bought those, because Uncle didn't and we were hungry. *I* looked after our meals."

"That was good of you, honey. Abby must not have liked it as much as you did; she was rail thin, but you were a solid little girl when you first came to live with Wanda. Neither of you wanted to sleep in your own bed, so you were put together in one bed, and you both wanted to stay up late."

"I know, Abby was afraid and I had to stay with her. We watched TV."

"Getting you two off to school was difficult. You both had missed school a lot, because of waking up late in the morning; you didn't have a day routine. Luckily, both of you were smart girls and caught up in school within the year." She smiled at her daughter.

Shayla looked at her mom with pride. "I had to take Abby to go to school for her grade one. Abby liked school, so I had to bring her every day, but I hated grade four."

"Yes, you helped her enormously, honey. Uncle also smoked in the house. You had asthma attacks and had an inhaler. You don't have asthma anymore. You knew already that Uncle was ill with heart disease, right? Can you imagine how awful it would've been for you girls, if Uncle Tim had died and you or Abby found him dead?" It seemed the proper moment to take Shayla's hand.

"Oh, never thought of that, but I do remember that I was worried a lot and never wanted Abby to be by herself at home with Uncle."

"Yes, you were really her little mother. When your mother was under suspicion of dealing drugs, she had the accident. Besides transporting them, we knew she was also using drugs – very good reasons to have you girls removed from her custody – and because she put someone in charge who wasn't adequate. That's not important anymore now; it's all ancient history, right?"

During the last sentences, Shayla's eyes had opened wide and she stared intently at Bernice, increasing the distance between them on the couch. "How do you know all of this? Like, I never saw any drugs, Mom."

"No, because you weren't living at her house, sweetheart; you were with Tim. Your birth mom – that sounds so strange; let's call her by her name, okay?" Shayla nodded, leaning forward, eager for her mom to continue. "Nora had a business address where she lived and met with her associates – she worked for suspected gang members – and she travelled a lot to the south and across the border, was probably trafficking.

I don't exactly remember everything and never heard all the details of the police investigation."

Shayla eyes were glued to Bernice's mouth, drinking in every word; she had moved to the edge of the couch. Bernice stopped talking and looked at her intently. "Are you feeling alright, honey? Should I stop talking?" She reached over and grabbed her daughter's other hand, holding it tightly, but Shayla pulled it free.

Shayla's eyes were narrowing and her eyebrows formed a deep groove on her forehead; she looked with suspicion in her eyes at Bernice. "No, don't stop, but it's so hard to believe. That's not at all what I remember. Like, how come you didn't tell me that before? I want to know everything!"

"Other social workers did he investigation, and the police gathered their own evidence. Nora opposed the removal, but the judge had seen enough and approved foster care for you two. My office got the file when that all was completed and you two were placed in foster care. If you want to see all that history, we could ask for your file through the information and privacy act. When you reach the legal age in a year, you'll get a copy of everything in that file. I can get you an application form from my office." Bernice was all business now – on familiar territory.

"No, Mom; I'm cool; you can tell me, please, like, I'd rather hear it from you, right? What else happened? Why didn't she visit us?"

"That was another problem; I wanted her to. Do you remember her visit with you both at my office? She was yelling and screaming, demanding to take you both outside to the park by herself. You got an asthma attack in the middle of it, probably aggravated by. You were barely able to breathe."

"I do remember that. Omigod, I'd forgotten all about that. What happened after?"

"She finally settled and you had a nice visit, Nora reading stories to you both, but she simply wouldn't have any more visits. She said she'd only visit with her children, if I let her have visits at her house, alone."

"We thought we would see her again."

Her expression had changed to sadness and Bernice touched her hand.

"I'm so sorry that couldn't happen, honey. You and Abby had been in foster care before. Nora managed to get you back when another social worker believed she had stopped using drugs. You're right, Nora was a strong and fearsome woman, and yes, she could be very scary."

Sadness on her face, Shayla leaned back and shook her head. "Wow, Mom, I can't believe all this. I don't remember having been at a foster home before Wanda. Crazy. I remember that I was always a bit afraid of her. Her voice was very loud, right?"

Bernice sat back too, now that the worst was over, and with kindness, smiled at her daughter. "Yes, I could hear her as far as my office when she was still at the reception; I was a bit afraid of her too, but I'm sure she loved you and Abby very much. That's why she did the right thing, letting you come into foster care, and by not being around you, although that still might be hard for you to accept. Think about this: She was a smart woman and knew her life was bad for children."

"But we wanted our mother."

She stroked Shayla's head and with a soft voice replied: "Of course you did; all children want their mother. She thought she had made arrangements that were good enough: Tim as caregiver, and once in a while dropping in on you both with presents. But did you know her?

Would it have been enough for you?" She stroked Shayla's hand lying slack inside her own hand.

"I wanted her to come way more often."

Shayla's sad expression broke Bernice's heart, and her own eyes welled up. "Right. You didn't get a chance to know her from those few visits. You both needed more to grow up." Bernice wanted to say something, but stopped, to give her daughter space to process all this news.

"Omigod, that's so sad; I feel sorry for Nora. Do you think she might have wanted to change, get off drugs? Like, if she hadn't been killed in the accident? And what about my birth dad? Where was he with all this?"

Bernice hesitated slightly before she continued, her steady gaze on Shayla's face. "Gabriel was deep into his addictions. I spoke a few times with him; he was also smart about the whole situation and said he was in no shape to look after children. He visited a few times at the office and at Wanda's after Nora died. Do you remember that?"

"Yes, I do remember some things about him. He was nice and quiet, sort-of-sad, right? He had this long black hair over his shoulders. I thought he looked sort of cool."

"I'll tell you a bit more, but you must let me know if you want me to stop."

"Yes, I will, Mom. Go on."

"He was heartbroken and hadn't seen Nora in years, and was living in another part of the province on a farm, until your placement in foster care. As far as I could see, he was a caring man, dealing with his relapse into addiction, very aware he had no ability to look after children."

She let go of Shayla's hand, who relaxed a bit and pulled a leg underneath her, leaning back in her seat. Her eyes were wide open, pupils narrowed and her cheeks flushed. "Why don't we take a break and let it sink all in for a bit; what do you say, Shayla?"

"Okay, then. I'll catch you some other time, cool. I will think about that email, right? I'll let you read it before I'll send it, okay?"

"That's great, honey."

It was Bernice who wanted the break. How was a child supposed to take all that sad family information? She herself had been affected, first by Nora's verbal aggression, by her treats, and then witnessing the children go through an emotional roller coaster after Nora's death.

Another issue that Shayla needed to hear in the future was their familial mental health issues. The research wasn't clear about the cause of mental health problems for foster children; was it the disrupted attachment to a parent with the mayhem and neglect of the addict's life, or was it the genetic heritage? Nurture or nature. She looked at Shayla, who sat quietly on the couch, staring at the floor.

Bernice pulled an arm through Shayla's and got up, hauling her daughter up to standing.

"Let's get an iced tea. How was the sleep over? Did you have a good time with the girls?" Shayla's face turned sweet and a glimmer settled in her eyes, but she didn't speak. "Let me give you a big hug. This was all awful to hear. Remember, you've got nothing at all to blame yourself for. I'm sure Nora and Gabriel loved you very much, and most importantly for you to know now, Dad and I both love you and Abby so very much too. Nothing you might do could change that – ever. You're a wonderful young lady and you can be whatever you set your mind to. You've already risen above the past, sweetheart. You're graduating soon." She pulled Shayla tightly against her and held her for a moment or two.

Shayla hugged her back and relaxed in her mom's arms. "I love you too, Mom." Bernice let her go. She smelled something unusual in Shayla's hair, but could not identify it. She assumed it was the laundry detergent Ellen's mom used. "We had a great time, Mom. Ellen's mom likes it when friends are visiting. Ellen hates being home alone. You know, she wants to do have another sleepover soon and her mother doesn't mind."

"Sure, honey; let me know when; I'm glad that you've got such good friends. I never had the opportunity myself for sleep overs; my parents were too strict."

———————

The boys were back. They announced their arrival with much shouting and whoops of "We won!" and the sound of gear bags being thrown into the laundry room adjacent to the kitchen, before they entered the kitchen. "Hi, Mom. We won the game with five nil from the Westside Warriors. What do you say about your boy now, hey? Daniel scored a goal." Jonathan came bouncing into the kitchen and gave his sister a punch on the arm.

"Ouch, don't do that, brat," she said and punched him back. Tom and Daniel joined them in the kitchen.

"It was a very good game," said Tom. "Even after you went back on a promise, I'm glad you made me go today. I forgive you, but don't you forget that you owe me a trade. I totally enjoyed watching that game. We've got some nice soccer talent living under our roof, Bernice. I am thinking of sending them to soccer camp this year, what do you think? Can we afford that? It's at the end of July, early August. We'd have to register now. We don't have any vacation plans, so this would be a good year for it."

Tom looked happy and relaxed; he walked over to Bernice and gave her a peck on the cheek, touching her shoulder and giving a gentle squeeze. She turned to him and kissed him back. Bernice's eyes searched Tom's face and eyes for information. Nothing; this wasn't not going to be easy. What was he up to? Will he stay home tonight?

When one child after the other opened the fridge door and after a quick look, closed it again, she wondered how they could be hungry again after their fast food binge. She smiled. "How come you guys are hungry? Didn't you go for hamburgers, as you usually do on Saturdays?" Bernice inquired, curious.

"Dad had to go back to the office and was in a hurry." Daniel said: "Do you have anything here? We can make our own. Don't worry, I know how to light the barbecue; Dad taught me," he added.

Bernice glanced at Tom's face again; still nothing there. "What's so important that you have to leave your family on a Saturday, Tom?"

"Oh, nothing much. That client from Vancouver wanted to see a few properties, so I made arrangements for a few showings. It won't take long. I'll be back by dinnertime. What are we having tonight?"

"I was thinking that whole salmon that you got from someone and is still sitting in the freezer. We've got to eat it soon before the new catch comes along. I could let it thaw in cold water; it'll be fine for tonight."

"Yes, that sounds nice. Let's do that. I'll be off. See you later." He planted a hasty kiss on Bernice's nose, and he was gone, just like that.

Jonathan came up with a box of frozen mini hamburgers and mini buns from the freezer. "Mom, can we have those sliders you got here?" Bernice sighed, not so much for Jonathan's question as for Tom's departure.

"Okay then. They can be cooked from frozen and the buns will thaw on the bread rack. Never mind lighting the barbecue, I'll do that. Give me that lighter, please." She took the lighter from Daniel. "When your dad is here to supervise, you can do it with him."

"Oh, Mom, you're such a spoil sport," he complained with a smile. Bernice thought that her son was right, she felt like a stick in the mud. It all fell back on her; she'll have to do everything. Usually, Tom gladly fulfilled his father role, teaching the boys the manly things, like cooking on the barbecue. She made a bargain; if he comes back in time tonight for dinner and does not leave again, they will be okay. If he leaves after dinner, or didn't come back for dinner, their marriage is in deep trouble, and she would have to address it with him.

"Okay, boys, get the condiments, buns, and the butter out on the deck and some plates and cutlery and let's have lunch. Jonathan, you can find Shayla and tell her we're having lunch. Don't bother looking for Abby; she is playing with her friend next door."

CHAPTER 12

L ying on top of her bed, eyes closed and relaxing with the whole afternoon ahead of her, Shayla imagined feeling Eric's lips on hers and reveled in the sweetness of it all. Last night, her feelings were strong, but she didn't think she had been stoned; she was just a passionate girl discovering what love was. Like a curious kitten observed a mouse, she approached her first experience slowly, carefully batting at it with a paw, to learn its effect.

She wondered what made people want to get close to someone. Was that love or lust? What attracted her about Eric? Was it his good temper, or his friendly and kind ways? Even as a basketball player, he certainly wasn't a jock. She hated those types, full of themselves and making her feel insecure and unattractive. Eric liked her; he said so. He didn't mind that she was only an adopted child. Oh, how confusing love and sex were. How did anybody know what to do, what to think, whom to trust? Could she trust Eric, or would he soon get tired of her and move on to a more attractive girl?

Suppose she had genes in her that make her act like her dad, or like her mom, and things went bad. What would happen, if he walked away from her? The image of Nora's pale face in the casket appeared, clearly dead, with make-up. She could see that it was her mother and yet, the face wasn't; there she was, a wax sculpture dressed like her mom with neat hair. She recalled that day, not knowing where she belonged, the long wait for her mom to come home over. How could she have left her daughters? How could she have all these people around her that said they were her family, and not even bother with occasionally saying hello in a phone call to her real family, her and Abby? What a mean thing to do.

The old feeling of utter loneliness seeped back in. Tears welled up and streamed over her cheeks, like a gentle, warm waterfall from a one-inch drop-off in a small creek in mid-summer. She let them fall freely, wasn't trying to stop or hold them back; the tears belonged to her. Why had this happened to her? She heard Bernice's words again and repeated them softly, like a prayer, a spell. Nothing really to do with me. I've got nothing to blame myself for. She surely had not deserved that.

Nora's ghastly image morphed into an approximation of Gabriel's face. She faintly remembered the handsome, dark stranger, who had given her his genes, who had made love to her mom – the wicked woman – who probably drugged him and then discarded him like a bag of garbage. The thought of seeing Gabriel soon was comforting; her heart lifted, imagining having a dad of the same blood, and her tears dried up. He'd be nice and gentle, and stick around this time; she would *make* him stay. They would surely get along.

Did Mom mean it for her to know her birth dad, or would Bernice and Tom get angry with her, give her the cold shoulder? The usual distrust poisoned her thoughts, like a chemical spill choking off all life in a wild stream. She would have to convince them they'd nothing to worry about, that she'd keep loving them and be a good daughter, even if eventually she would leave them to live with Gabriel. What if she failed? If she left home to start living with Gabriel, she'd have to take Abby with her and look after her too; she could do that, she was strong.

When Uncle was sick, she'd grab some money from his pocket and went to the McDonald's, a few blocks away. With a shock she realized she hadn't been worried about Abby for a long time, because Bernice had done that for her. Forcing her thoughts away from the darkness to turn to goodness, she softly repeated her mantra: Nothing really to do with me. I've done nothing to blame myself.

Could she trust herself? She remembered the dressing room, the nice top, putting it on and pulling on her own sweater over top, leaving the dressing room, and leaving the store. Sudden sweat prickled on her brow and under her hair in her neck. Maybe she *was* like her mom, maybe she was no good; she had Nora's genes in her. She couldn't cry anymore; she had run out of tears.

She got up from her bed. Her pillowcase was damp. She stripped it from her pillow and hung the empty cover over the edge of her plastic desk chair, stripped her clothes off and entered the bathroom. She drew a hot bath and poured some lavender beads into it. She slipped in the tub into the healing fragrance, enjoying the warmth enveloping her body.

What was she going to do next year? Where will she be; *who* will she be? Will she succeed? She couldn't leave home yet, as she didn't know where to start. Besides dancing, she had no idea where her strengths were, and what subjects to take in college. The calendars and courses were so confusing, and how was she going to make a choice? It was beyond her.

She probably should work for a few years before going to college. She'd have to fill herself with skills and good thoughts first before everything. Right now, she was nothing – a person in an empty shell. She had nobody, and her heart was empty. Who would want her like this? Slowly, her eyes closed and she dreamt of Eric.

CHAPTER 13

Bernice was preparing dinner – the girls in their bedrooms and the boys playing video games in the downstairs family room – when Tom called. She swallowed and straightened her shoulders, intent on recklessly demanding his presence at dinner; she wanted, no, needed to see where that would lead, and whether blowing a bit of wind would break that bough. She walked to her bedroom, gently closed the door behind her and answered the phone. "Hi, honey, what's up?"

"Hey, Bernie, what're you up to? Have you planned dinner yet? If you did, sorry, don't count on me. My clients are close to making an offer, but want to further discuss a reasonable price, so we're going to have a few drinks together; I'll offer them a dinner as well. I hope to write up the offer and have it in the bag before the end of the weekend."

"That's too bad, Tom. I really need to talk to you and don't want to postpone it any longer. I'm worried about us. We haven't had any time together in weeks, just you and me. I wonder what's up with you. Tom, let me be up front with you. I'm beginning to wonder: Are you having an affair?" It came out just like that. She hadn't exactly intended to say that, but there was no turning back now.

The answer came immediately, smoothly, and with sufficient indignation. "Honey, how could you think that? I'm busting my butt to get some sales going and you wonder about my loyalty? I'll always be loyal to you and the kids. Family comes first; you know that!"

She held her breath for the whole time it took Tom to answer her – at least ten seconds – then took a deep breath. "That's still no answer, Tom. Are you having an affair?"

"Jeez, Bernice! What makes you think that? I'm disappointed you could think that about me. I'd never think that of you."

He was using the counter-attack diversion method; she was pushing forward, now 90% sure her instincts were right. Of course she wouldn't have an affair – she was too damn busy. "Tom, I need an answer, please." Her voice was made of steel, like her will.

"Bernice, if I did, I wouldn't discuss that on the phone, but no, to answer you, I'm not having an affair. I'm just calling you to tell you I won't be home for supper. I'll talk to you when I get home. I have to go now. My people are waiting." He spoke too many words, creating a vast distance between them in those few seconds before he disconnected.

Tom gave the answer she hoped to hear, but he hadn't convinced her; the poison of suspicion churned up her stomach, as if he had indeed replaced her. Thinking of eating made her feel sick. Now that she had opened the door with the question, he might start thinking about starting one – if he didn't already have a lover. Was she pushing him towards another woman?

She'd heard from friends about affairs, but never considered it a possibility in their relationship. Tom had somehow become smaller, softer, less macho, his personality less attractive, and most of all, he seemed to have lost his devotion to her. She must have at least partly caused this decline, or why was his focus elsewhere? He still was ever so friendly and popular with their friends and his business associates, as far as she could tell. She had to admit she didn't admire and trust him the same as when they first met, and it seemed mutual; his sex drive was gone – at least with her. Was it her fault? Had she lost the qualities– whatever they were – that had attracted him? Feeling the acid rise in her oesophagus after a few bites, she stopped eating the spaghetti with a mild tomato sauce, but the kids liked it.

After dinner with the children, she called a friend. Kate was a co-worker on a different team, who had divorced her unfaithful husband, and since then had little trust in any man. Bernice knew Kate's next partner well. Beth was a police officer, occasionally assisting at the scene of a difficult home visit with an aggressive parent, or when police stumbled on children during a parent's arrest., so Kate's advice to Bernice was predictable: "Get to the bottom of it and trust your instincts. Most unhappy men never have the gumption to leave a woman before they've found a potential replacement. You might want to check whether he's looking, or maybe even found someone."

"How would one do that?"

"Well, you could get hold of his cell phone, or check his email. I don't want to be insensitive, but I have some news about Beth and me."

"What's the news?"

"Now that we've been together for ten years, we're thinking about getting married. That's long enough to be sure." She giggled. "I think it'll be a public event." Bernice knew she referred to their high profile in the local GLBTQ organization and the monthly dances.

"That's great news. I think you two are a good match."

"Does finding a new partner before replacing the old girl apply to women as well?"

"I'm not sure. I don't think so; women can talk about these things. You should lighten up a bit; you work to much."

"Yeah, you're right. I don't know that I could snoop on Tom; it's so dishonest. I'm more for the direct approach. But enough about that. I always wondered: What brought you and Beth together?

"I didn't know then I could go for a woman, and I don't know now, what exactly to call me, but women were always closer to me than men, so it never felt weird to me that I liked Beth when she took the initiative to try me out a little closer. She called in a worker at an arrest and removed a couple of kids together, and we went out for a drink. To make a short story even shorter: I found out that Beth was the right kind of love for me. *You* also need some fun, girlfriend!"

"Yes, I should lighten up. I used to be a fun-loving woman." That admission didn't make her feel any better.

At 10 p.m. Tom wasn't home yet. Bound by the promise to herself, Bernice went to work on a strategy. She couldn't think about anything else, realizing she didn't know anything about Tom. She wasn't sure which restaurant Tom was having dinner with his guests, and wasn't even sure he was actually working. She could call him on his cell, but he could not answer, or worse, lie. If she'd known where he was, she'd have left home and checked him out and his company. Oh, no, this meant she was becoming a stalker.

She couldn't wait any longer; maybe she'd find something on his computer. When she walked by Shayla's bedroom on her way to Tom's den, she noticed a strip of light underneath her door; why was she still up? She'd worry about Shayla later. She sat down behind the laptop to open Tom's emails. Damn; he had a password. She would have to be smarter. She considered it his laptop, although she had her own user profile on it.

She switched users, logged in, waited till her profile came up and opened the Internet browser. She typed: Private Detectives. According to what came up, this service apparently was now called Private Investigators: A list popped up with a number of options. She picked one and clicked. Photos of obviously compromising situations popped up, examples of situations in which customers had hired this company. A short video clip showed a couple at a motel, both looking over their shoulder, about to enter the room, the man inserting a key into the door, with the heading: Is your spouse having an affair? Let us find out the truth. Free Consult. Wow, exactly what she wanted. She made a note of the address and phone number of a couple of P.I.s and resolved to hire someone the next workday.

Curious, she typed in some other words: What to do when your spouse is cheating. Gosh, really, there's a website for that too! She read: Don't make any major decisions about ending your marriage now, just because your spouse has been unfaithful. Your feelings are neither right nor wrong. Talk to a counsellor. Take care of yourself. Take it one day at the time – borrowed from the Twelve Steps Alcohol Recovery program. Her eyes glued to the screen, she found a wealth of information at her fingertips about a subject she didn't know a thing about, beyond custody battles in court. She realized that reading up on what to expect would save some money on counsellors later. Luckily, she had an employment assistance plan. She bookmarked the sites she found most useful.

When she heard the front door open softly, she logged off from her user profile, and waited. Funny he wouldn't open the garage door. She heard Tom sneak through the house towards the stairs in his socked feet; his soft footfalls moved towards the den. He abruptly stopped by the den door with his shoes in one hand when he spotted Bernice behind the computer, his eyes wide, his posture straight.

"Hi, what are you doing behind my computer…?" His voice turned up and then trailed off while he looked around for a place to sit; since Bernice was sitting in his desk chair, he decided to use the ottoman.

"Hi to you, too. I thought this was a family computer," she retorted, more briskly than intended. "I needed to look something up tonight and didn't want to wait." She couldn't look him in the eye and pretended to be busy with logging off; she slapped the laptop lid down.

"Sure, of course," his voice was now devoid of any emotion. He seemed on edge, jiggling one foot.

"How did it go tonight," she began, making an effort to keep her own voice light and businesslike.

"What are you referring to?" He was too cautious; he looked like a trapped fox looking for an opening in the fence of the henhouse. She wondered how reliable her observations were and decided to first collect more information before she would confront him again. She looked at his face that was closed now – no emotion whatsoever visible.

"Well, did you close? The negotiations at dinner; you said you were confident about closing the sale tonight."

"I thought you'd be in bed by now," he replied. "I didn't think you'd stay up for me. How were the boys for you tonight? Did they behave?" Tom looked her in the eye for a very brief second, then looked around the office, as if he had entered it for the very first time.

"Oh, the boys were fine. Why are you stalling, Tom? Let me guess, the sale fell through." Her voice was still light while she kept her gaze on him. He finally looked at her.

"Well, to tell you the truth, yes, they ended up not making the offer. It's frustrating, when you work hard for a customer and they just take the free dinner and walk off. But, what can you do? In this market one has to take every opportunity to try to make the sale. Let's hope they'll come back tomorrow after sleeping on it."

"Good thing I've got a steady job with a pension, right?" Bernice couldn't help herself, something edgy was raised in her. Tom had the potential to make twice her income, or more in a good year, but the lean years were bad. "Well, hang in there; the market will turn around," she added, to soften her previous statement. She was dead-tired all of a sudden. "Let's go to bed; it's late," she added, getting up from the desk chair and making her way out of the den, past Tom.

"You go ahead; I'll check my email." She knew he would stay down, until he was sure she'd be asleep. She could read him like one of her children.

———

The next morning, Bernice closed her office door as soon as she arrived, started dialing the number of one of the Private Investigators and made an appointment for noon that same day. She desperately needed somebody on her side and ran her plans by Kate, who approved her strategy. Shortly before noon, she walked to the investigator's office, tense, and aware she was on the threshold of some unknown world; she intended to keep her meeting short and businesslike.

The office receptionist seemed efficient, and the company's office was clean and tastefully decorated, the investigator's credentials (retired police officer) adequate, and she gave it all a passing grade, in spite of the somewhat sleazy nature of the task assigned. The brown-skinned, middle-aged man with a slightly protruding stomach underneath his baby-blue sweater, appeared from an office, came towards her, smiling, offered his hand, and after shaking hers, pointed at his office, a few yards down the corridor. "Shall we?"

She provided the necessary details, insisting he'd call her by her first name. After less than twenty minutes she left his office, satisfied with the procedure. During the afternoon, a blend of excitement and fear kept her stomach tightened that had started last night and didn't abate all day

———

Within a week, Bernice heard back from the P.I. She made an appointment for Friday afternoon after work; that way she wouldn't have to return to her office, in case she needed some time for recovery – depending on the news. That Friday she left work and drove to the P.I. office, parked in the nearby parking garage, and walked the block to his office. As she dragged her body across the street – the weight of the world on her shoulders – her footfalls sounded heavy, as if her soles were sticking to the pavement. She wasn't ready, all of a sudden was sorry for her action; she simply couldn't hear the outcome, wasn't willing to face what she'd started. Her heart was racing; in spite of the cool day, she was perspiring.

She entered the P.I.'s office. Her hands were shaky; she stretched them in front of her and studied them. Maybe she needed to eat something; her blood sugar might be low. She dug around in her purse, found a granola bar and ate it with a dry mouth. She needed a drink. She got up and walked to the water cooler in the corner of the waiting room. Just as she was swallowing a tiny cup of water, the investigator arrived and greeted her in a cordial manner.

"Hi, Bernice. How are you?"

"That's fine."

The man looked at her, smiled and nodded, gesturing his hand toward his office. They walked in and sat down, each on the proper side of his desk. "I know that these situations aren't easy and the quicker the results are known, the better. I'll get to the point. Don't you agree?" Yes, dink. Get on with it then! She nodded, unable to speak. The man opened a large brown envelope and laid out a series of photos before her on his desk. She glanced at them, then she swallowed hard and noticed she was still thirsty, so she drank her water.

"I'll need some more water, sorry." She got up and refilled her paper cup in the reception, returned, and sat down, forcing her eyes down to the photos to absorb what she had seen in a glance and couldn't take in, a few seconds earlier. The first photo showed Tom holding an extremely pretty young woman by the elbow, guiding her up the exterior stairs of a building. Bernice immediately recognized Tom's receptionist. The woman was leaning into him, her head on his shoulder.

The next photo showed the couple kissing passionately in a restaurant or bar, a place unfamiliar to Bernice. Her heart beat skipped and started beating again more intensely; she could feel its pulsing in her neck. She was extremely cold, wishing she'd brought a warmer jacket.

She looked at photo number three. She saw an unfamiliar home and the couple about to go inside; Tom had one arm around the woman who had both her arms around his neck, while Tom reached with a key in his other hand to open the front door. No mistake possible: They were really into each other. Damn, it was true. Bernice got up and said in a voice, shakier than she anticipated: "Is that all then? What do I owe you?"

The dick replied: "It's always a shock to people when they see the proof. I'm sorry. There's more. Do you want to know the name and address? I do have all of that information, as well as dates and times and locations of their meetings."

Bernice nodded her head, fighting back the tears. The man shoved the photos back into the envelope together with a typed list of names and dates, handed it to her and replied with a business-like voice. "That's $1500. We only needed three evenings of surveillance, before we got the results. You can pay with credit card, Interac, or cash, if you like."

Bernice paid with her credit card and hurried out of the agency. She managed to walk to the nearby park without crying, dropped herself on a bench by the pond and covered her face with her hands. She wept, silently, tears streaming down her chin, dripping to the gravel from underneath her hands. Thoughts jumbled through her head: I should have never started this. What's the price of the truth? The bastard. What am I going to do? How demeaning. After a while, she calmed down. She got out her cell phone and called Kate.

"Hi, Kate, I've got the results. Can you meet with me? I can't go home. Can I sleep at your place tonight?" Her voice said it all – thin and soft.

"Of course you can, honey. I'll come and get you. I'll make up some excuse to tell Beth. She's not the jealous type, anyway. Where are you?" While waiting for Kate, Bernice called Tom's office. He was not in: What a surprise. She called his cell, and his voice mail clicked in: Leave a message. Even better. She would leave him in charge. Her message said she wasn't coming home, he would have to look after the kids, and that she would call him in the morning.

When Kate drove up to the curb by the park entrance, she texted. Getting up from the park bench, Bernice's knees shook; she held on to the backrest to get to standing. In Kate's car, she burst out in tears again, sharing the bad news between her sobs, almost incomprehensible to Kate.

Driving, Kate couldn't do anything else, but grab Bernice's hand. "It's okay, Bernice, let it out, it's okay." By the time they arrived at the home, Bernice had stopped sobbing and could breathe again.

Her friends lived in a small home in a former industrial section of the city transformed into a gentrified, artsy district. Theirs was a cute and colourful house with a white picket fence and a front garden full of blooming flowers, growing exuberantly in British cottage style in spite of the early season. Once inside, Beth joined them in the entrance and asked whether she could do anything to help, but before she could say anything, Kate replied for her.

"Could I ask you to make the dinner tonight by yourself, while Bernice and I sit in the back yard and talk some more?"

"Okay, Kate, no problem. You girls go ahead and take your time."

They sat quietly in the pretty back yard. "What are you going to do, Bernice?" asked Kate after a while.

"I've got no idea, I can't think. I only know I just can't face Tom, but tomorrow I'll have to. What do you think about this all? Tom says I always over-react. Am I overreacting?"

"No, I don't think that at all. I'm not sure what to think. Cheating is supposedly more frequent in the GLBT world, probably because our partnerships were not sanctioned by marriage vows until recently. We have the name to be more promiscuous, although I don't agree at all with that reputation. I'll be devastated if I found out that Beth cheated on me."

"I'm so hurt he's lying straight to my face. How could he? Was our whole marriage a lie? I feel I don't know him. I'll have to face I'm married to a stranger. Tom doesn't want to be with me anymore, but can't tell me that. Instead, he goes behind my back and seduces a twenty-something-year-old. What do I tell our children?" A tear found its path down her cheek; she impatiently wiped it away.

Kate reached over and took her hand. "I believe we only see part of our mate, even at the best of times, and we often don't know what goes on inside our partner's head. You've started the work of talking about it; you can be proud of that. Your marriage doesn't automatically have to end here, Bernice; you're just upset now. It's important to keep talking to each other and share your thoughts and feelings. You both have a busy life; do you still make time for each other?"

The tears kept coming. Bernice wiped her face with both hands and straightened her back. "Yes, you're right. We don't spend any time together; that's why I was concerned. We got caught up in our lives, our work, and the children. My life seems all about duties and we do hardly any fun things anymore. I can't remember when I did something for myself I really wanted to do."

"Bernie, let's look at this in rational way. This is the first time that Tom cheated on you, or did you have any suspicions before? If each marriage ended when one of the partners turned to another, we wouldn't have many marriages left."

"But Kate, this is *my* marriage, not just any marriage. Show some compassion." Bernice looked at Kate with resentment.

"Yes, I know, sorry. I'm too practical sometimes. Being cheated on is devastating, and I'm sorry this happened to you. I know what that's like. But really, you'll get over it. It depends on what you and Tom will do, now the cat is out of the bag. Listen, I was curious myself and looked into the marriage and divorce rates, in preparation for our plans to marry. The stats say almost 50 percent of straight marriages end anyway, so the other fifty succeed, right?"

With Kate's eyes on her, she listened to what else Kate would come up with, reminding herself her friend meant well. Kate slowly went on. "Honey, you're going through a rough patch. Also this will pass. Roughly 30 to 60 percent of all married individuals will engage in infidelity at some point during their marriage and often it's a reason for divorce, but some couples do get over it."

"Tell me something I don't know."

"So, it comes down to what staying in the marriage is worth to *you*, and of course, how long that fling lasts, and what she means to Tom. If you can wait it out until that affair ends –because it will end – you don't need to get divorced. You know that, don't you? Of course, you could ask that he'd stop seeing her."

Bernice nodded, keeping her eyes on Kate. "I wished I was more like you, so damn practical and analytical, while my heart bleeds and I'm falling apart. It just hurts so much. I can't trust my best friend, the father of my children. Why couldn't he have a virtual fling? And then with that child – she's not much older than Shayla. How insulting, and also creepy." She wept softly again.

Kate grabbed the tissue box and placed it beside Bernice. "Want a glass of wine, Bernie?" she asked gently. They talked for a while longer, enjoying a glass of wine, until Beth set the food on the kitchen counter and called for Kate and Bernice to come and serve themselves. They ate the chicken stir fry dinner at the island counter. Beth was curious, but didn't ask any questions and kept a light conversation going, sharing meaningful glances with Kate and some gestures that Bernice didn't notice; she was quiet, deep in thought.

After dinner, Bernice wanted to disappear; she couldn't stand the intimacy of the couple anymore. "Could I borrow a pair of PJs and do you have an extra toothbrush? I'm tired and want to lie down for a bit, if that's okay. I wonder how they're making out at home." Right then, her cell phone rang; Shayla was calling. "I'm going to take that in the guest room," Bernice explained and quickly left the room.

———

"Hi, sweetheart, what's up?"

"Where *are* you, mom; what are you doing? Dad says you're not coming home? Why not?"

"I need some time for me. I can't get into details, Shayla; it's between Dad and me. You might want to help Dad with the boys. Are you good for the night, or did you have plans? I'll come home tomorrow." She hoped Tom wouldn't leave Shayla to babysit; that would be wrong under the circumstances. In a way, her absence forced him to take on more childcare responsibilities. Serves him right.

"No, I'm fine, but could you let me have a stay-over on Saturday? Ellen wants me to come over." Her voice was quite high, different, but Bernice didn't notice it, until later.

"Sure, honey, that's fine. Thanks for helping out Dad tonight. See you tomorrow then. I love you."

"Thanks, mom. Love you too."

CHAPTER 14

Shayla wondered why everyone coming through the mall's entrance doors stared at her. She repositioned her feet every few minutes, changing her stance, a few feet from the entrance inside the mall, while waiting for Ellen and Anita. She glanced at her cell phone – no texts. She tried to decide to wait in the food court and get a pop, instead of being exposed to the judgment of a bunch of shoppers, but stayed put anyway.

She needed an outfit for later that night; she wanted to look good for Eric. She spent her cash on cigarettes and shoes, so couldn't ask her mom for an advance on babysitting fees – under the circumstances. Her mom had called her to help with the boys and agreed to the overnight at Ellen's, without putting her through the usual third degree. She came home early in the morning looking weird, her face swollen and her eyes avoiding hers. Something was going on between her parents. Shayla had stared at her, but didn't ask what happened, afraid for the answer. With enough troubles of her own, she didn't want to think about her mom's problems.

She looked at her phone again: Jeez, not even a text! Her friends were always late, but not Shayla – she was always too early. She didn't know why she did that. She hated being such a chicken, never standing up for herself, always trying to please everybody. She should toughen up, starting right now; they damn-well could text her to catch up. She wandered deeper into the mall into the designer brand outlet section. She might as well look for something to wear and entered the Le Chateau, closest to the food court. She pushed the hangers from right to left, critically inspecting each garment that passed her eyes, until she hit a multi-coloured dress with a short, wide skirt and a draped top with transparent shoulders and sleeves. It was a dream, elegant and very sexy. She grabbed another, similar dress, but in a different style.

Two young sales clerks were chatting by the till, not watching her. She entered a dressing room with both dresses, put on the first dress and looked in the mirror over her shoulder to see her backside. It hid all of her flaws – a generous butt, wide hips – and showed off her long legs. Perfect.

She examined the front view. Her smallish breasts looked quite substantial with the draped material gathered asymmetrically crossed across her torso, accentuating that area. She would have to wear a low cut bra, as the top of her breasts would be visible through the gauzy, delicate lace. Her mom would think it too glamorous, but she could always wear it again to the year-end grad parties, coming up. She simply must have the dress. She looked at the price tag. Whoa, that was steep!

Without a second of reflection she ripped off the security tag, which wouldn't come off easily; she had to pry her nail file underneath the electronic fob to wrest if from its bottom, and slip it off the dress' sleeve. She threw it under the bench of the change room and got dressed, putting her own clothes over top of the dress. Luckily she was wearing her loose, hippy dress that covered all. She put on her coat, grabbed her purse off the bench, got the dress she didn't want and the empty hanger, walked out of the change area holding the rejected dress in front of her. She hung it and the empty hanger on the designated garment rack outside the dressing rooms.

She looked around and caught a glimpse of the store girls – still chatting by the till – who glanced back at her for a few seconds, but were not making any attempts to move from their perch, or to speak to her. They returned to their conversation – this customer wasn't buying.

Shayla marched towards the food court. She still didn't see her friends. Her whole shopping spree had only taken ten minutes, at the most. She wondered whether they'd said to meet at the other end of the mall, by the coffee shop. Yes, maybe that was it. She hadn't been paying much attention to their chatter, not feeling so much part of their clan these days.

Overdressed and hot, sweat prickling in the back of her neck, she decided to walk to the other end of the mall through the outdoor route. That was a big mistake. She opened one of the double doors and stepped outside the mall, eager to get away from the store, when she felt a hand grab her right shoulder, holding it with such power that it forced her body to turn sideways.

She saw a large, red-faced, sweaty Caucasian man in a rumpled suit, barking something at her. She had trouble hearing him, her heart beating two hundred times a minute, a whistling sound in her ears. It was suddenly very bright outside and her knees where weak under her. "Excuse me?" she asked politely, trying to wriggle her shoulder free from his stealthy grip.

The burly ogre put his face close to hers. "You heard me; you're just stalling. Give me an answer, now," he said with a gruff voice with a British-sounding accent.

"What?" she tried again.

"You took something from the store that you didn't pay for, a dress. You must go with me to the store office. Shall I call the police, or are you willing to go with me? Your choice."

"Where will you take me?" Shayla asked in a quiet voice. Thoughts tumbled through her head in random order, making it hard to decide what to do: I'm going to miss Ellen and Anita. I won't have the dress. Will he arrest me? Omigod, I'm like Nora. What's Mom going to say? Dad will hate me. I won't get to see my other dad. No police!

"Well, what will it be, make up your mind. I don't have all day. To the office, so you can show me what you took, and of course, to talk." the man said in his funny accent. He wore an ear piece and a tiny microphone clipped to his collar.

"Yes, to the office." Her voice was wavering and she looked down, still trying to wiggle her body from his hold. She told herself she wasn't going to faint, but felt very, very sweaty, moisture building up in her waistline and between her breasts. She had no idea where the office might be.

The man turned back towards the store entrance holding her firmly by her shoulder in his iron grip; they went back inside the mall. Once inside, they walked towards a side door right beside the main entrance, a door she had never noticed before. PERSONNEL ONLY, it said.

They walked through a long corridor with many doors on either side, paint scuffed and discoloured to a poisonous green, at places coming right off the walls in wafer-thin patches; overhead blazed fluorescent lights. She heard his pants rustle against his legs as he slowly moved his large body forward in a sort of crabby walk, his right hand now gripping her upper arm. She could smell him, a greasy, musky smell like her brothers' guinea pig cage in need of cleaning.

He picked one of the doors and led her into a small office, practically bare with only a table and one chair behind it, two chairs on the other side, and a phone; he sat down heavily behind the desk, blocking the exit, and barked: "Hand me your purse and sit down."

Shayla didn't have any choice but to hand it over. To her consternation, he opened her handbag, turned it upside down and shook its contents out in front of her on the table. He then opened the zippered inside pockets and took out whatever was stored in there: Tylenol, tampons, lipstick, other cosmetics, a prescription bottle, cigarettes, a lighter, and a condom.

"What medication are you taking?" He pointed at the plastic vial.

"Antibiotics; I had an infection," she answered with a timid voice, a blush of shame covering her face for the condom.

"Are you using any other drugs?"

"No, why are you asking?" she said, feeling little braver. "I'm not a drug user. I am going to high school graduating this year. I'm a good girl."

"Have you shoplifted before?" He scrutinized her face.

"No," she lied, "this is my first time." More heat and sweat.

"Take your coat off. Then take that dress off that you took without paying. Sometimes we give people a break when we are in a good mood." His eyes roamed over her body as Shayla took her coat off. She felt naked and shivered.

"I believe you when you say you're a good girl. If you take that dress off now, you won't be sorry. I'm giving you a second chance here, young lady."

Some logical thought came to her: "How do you know it was me?"

"From the clerks; they checked the change room after you left and found the tag under the bench and an empty hanger on the rack beside it." He spoke his clarification in a softer voice with as much kindness as he could generate: "Our wireless system, you know. But, if you don't take the dress off, I'll have to turn you over to the police and if they decide to charge you, you'll have a record."

Shayla shivered and her hands started to shake; she didn't know what to do and looked at the security ogre with her eyes full of water, about to overflow. Finally, she managed to form a sentence. "Please, I'll do what you say, if you leave the room, please?" She spoke in her most polite voice, practically pleading.

The man seemed distracted, slowly raised a hand to his earpiece and pushed it closer into his ear with his big digit; he listened for a moment and started talking into his collar. "How many?" Pause. "I'm busy." Pause. "Right now?" Pause. "Okay, I'll be there in thirty seconds." He got up very quickly for such a large man and made his way out the room, turning back at the door to face her.

"You take that dress off and leave it here on the table, pack up your stuff and get out of here. I'd better not catch you at it again; next time you won't get off this easily. I'm needed upstairs." And he was gone.

Shayla couldn't believe her good fortune. She quickly undressed, threw the dress on the table, put on her own clothes, threw her things in her purse and ran through the corridor, out through the side door and into the bright daylight – as far away as she could from Le Chateau. Euphoria enveloped her and she whispered a thanks to whomever up there was on her side. It was just too embarrassing to tell the girls and would undo all the progress she had made. She wondered where that guy was before he grabbed her, as she never saw him lurking in the store.

When she reached the other side of the mall at the coffee shop, Ellen and Anita were browsing at the books and magazine racks adjacent to the coffee shop, each with a book in their hand that they dropped back on the table when they saw Shayla enter the store.

"Hey, where were you? We've been waiting for half an hour."

"Sorry, but I was waiting at the other end, when I realized we'd said to meet here. You could've texted me." She looked sideways at them, her head tilted, eyes accusatory; offence is the best defence.

Ellen shrugged. "Never mind. It's going to be so much fun tonight. Is Eric coming?" The girls wandered through the mall and chatted in rapid fire back-and-forth about the evening's upcoming adventures.

"Yes, he said he would; he texted me just this morning. Omigod I'm so excited. We might be doing it tonight. I think I'm ready, you know. Shit, he had a pack of condoms in his car last Wednesday; he showed them to me."

"Crazy. What did you say? I would've died."

"I didn't know what to say. My face must've been beet-red, right. But really, if you think about it, like, it's good of him to think about birth control; it's responsible, right? I like that about him, don't you?"

"I think it's great; like you said, it shows initiative, and he cares for you. Good for him," Anita answered. Ellen nodded her head.

"He gave me one for safekeeping, just in case he loses them or forgets them; sweet."

CHAPTER 15

That Friday night, Bernice had the children all farmed out for her talk with Tom. Shayla got her wish staying over at Ellen's. Although she wasn't sure about that decision, with Ellen's mom's parenting style so very different from hers – borderline neglectful, she'd call it – she had let her go. With a mostly absent mother, Ellen did pretty well whatever she liked. Never mind; she would have to let Shayla go at some point in her life. When your daughter hits seventeen, the time to practice letting go had arrived, she told herself.

They hadn't spoken since her night away; Tom hadn't asked any questions and she hadn't volunteered any explanations. The morning of her return, she simply asked for him to be home on Friday night, because she wanted to talk and show him something. She couldn't believe his charade of coolness – but he had looked guilty. "No problem, I'll make a point of being home at eight."

It was 7:30 p.m. now. She walked to the liquor cabinet, poured a glass of wine and had a word with herself about not drinking for courage. Her friends always teased her and told her they'd love to see her plastered for once in her life, often admonishing her to let loose while out together. She never did. That was just her, the cautious and responsible social worker, a bit of a control freak, although she couldn't really admit that. It was important to her to set an example, to put her money where her mouth was, so she would do her job with integrity – a world apart from some of her pregnant clients.

Despite her usual tolerance towards her clients, in her heart she couldn't accept Nora's assurances she had abstained during her pregnancies. Nora, the author of many literally incredible stories. Well, she'd better focus on her own problems now, but once landed on the mother track, she was unable to steer her thoughts away from her children.

Abby was less emotionally affected than Shayla. But then again, Shayla had been exposed a lot longer to Nora's parenting, or rather, non-parenting. After that unlucky start in life, the girls needed their two-parent family. She couldn't raise them without Tom, never mind raising four children alone. They simply must stay together. Her glass of wine disappeared fast. She heard the front door open and Tom's voice: "Hello, I'm home. Where are you?"

"I'm here, in the living room." She refilled her glass, got the earlier prepared snacks from the fridge and put the tray with crackers, cheese, pate, and some other finger food on the coffee table. Tom probably hadn't eaten yet. Neither had she, unable to get anything down. She felt sick to her stomach and another headache was starting to build.

Tom looked haggard, his hair disheveled, as if he had pulled his fingers through it repeatedly; it needed a shampoo. He slowly moved towards her, and standing beside her chair, gave her a peck on the cheek. "How's things? Where are the kids?"

"Out; this evening is for us. We have to talk. Thanks for coming home." She stiffly turned toward him to look at his face, but avoided his eyes.

"That sounds serious. Have you turned into a Lesbian?" His feeble attempt at humouring her fell flat: She resolved she wasn't going to make it easy for him this time and wasn't going to be charmed by his crappy jokes.

"Very funny. This might not be known in your circles, but it's not contagious, you know, although sometimes I wished I were gay. At least I can trust women."

He sat down across from her on the couch, not laughing. "What are you saying, Bernice, come out with it. What did you want to discuss?"

She inhaled deeply and released her breath very slowly, then threw the envelope with photos on the table and leaned back into her chair, willing herself to stay calm and especially, stay rational. "This is a set of photos, dates and names collected by somebody on my request. Why don't you have a look at it and see what you think? I'm very curious to hear an explanation of some kind. Convince me."

Stone-faced, Tom opened the manila packet and slid out its contents, grabbed the top sheet – a list of dates and places. He put it aside on the coffee table, then took the whole pile of photos all at once and turned them over, one by one. After inspection of each photo, he put it down on the table with slow, deliberate movements, as if inspecting pictures of a new listing, carefully and with intent, weighing the value of each photo.

Bernice tried to read his face, but there was nothing to read. Who was this man who could study his own betrayal in pictures and be unmoved? She wanted to scream, hit him, wanted to throw the vase of flowers on the coffee table at him, do anything to get a reaction from this cold-hearted being – her husband. But she didn't and made herself lean back in the chair, willing herself to stay calm by controlling her deep breaths, in and out, controlling her discomfort, like in yoga class.

"I see. You know, then. It must've cost you a bundle. How much? Did you really have to do that? Why didn't you ask?"

"I did ask," she calmly replied. "You lied and said not to be silly. Well, who's silly now?" Her voice started to crack.

"What do you want, Bernice?" His voice was like a knife, steeled and cold, lacking the emotion she hoped for. Anger rose in her chest, although she managed to make her voice sound to mirror his coldness. "I want you to stop that relationship."

He responded without a second of reflection. "That's not going to happen. I don't see what my friendship with Marla has to do with our relationship and our family. Having said that, I don't want you to worry. I'm not going to leave the kids without a father."

In the face of so much denial she was unable to contain herself and spoke louder now, frustrated, her voice demanding, although she felt like crying. "It has *everything* to do with our relationship. You cannot have both her and me. What happened to us that you have to flee into the arms of a teenager? Disgusting." She poured herself another glass of wine.

Tom got up. "Don't exaggerate; she's not a teen. Truthfully? You're still my best friend and always will be, but I lost the attraction I once had for you. You're the mother of my boys, but it's unreasonable to expect to be married and have sex with only one person for the rest of one's life. That is impossible and unnatural. It doesn't mean that we can't stay in a marriage and raise a family together." He looked up and she saw something soft in his eyes.

"Really? That's what you feel?"

"Many others manage rather successfully. You'll just have to leave me some space for my own pleasures, and I will leave you space for whatever you want. We're both adults. We can deal with this rationally, can't we?" Tom paced the room, like a professor lecturing his class.

Although becoming more agitated, and there was an edge to it now, his voice was still controlled, and he appeared calm.

Bernice didn't believe her ears, her eyes opened wide, and a cold feeling came over her. She got up as well and standing in front of him she responded in an octave higher than usual. "See, that's exactly the point. It can't be done. We're not raising the kids together. You're gone a lot of the time, counting on me for the kids. You promised me we'd raise Abby and Shayla together. And what about our boys? They need you too. When was the last time we went on vacation as a family?"

"Well, okay, I'll give you that. I've been away quite a bit lately. But that was truly work-related, although not all of it; I have to admit that. All work I do is or you, for the family, just like you. That's not all on me. How much time do you want me to spend with the kids? If you want me to follow a schedule, I'm all for it. Go ahead and make one; I'll make sure that it will jive with what I can deliver."

"Damn you! You speak about our marriage like it was a fucking business deal. How about this: You have hurt me so very deeply; nobody ever hurt me like this before. I love you and you destroyed my trust in you. How could you? Don't you love me anymore?"

Unable to hold back any longer, her body crumpled on the chair and she dissolved into sobbing. She buried her face in her hands, releasing more tears than she thought possible. Her lost love and her marriage drained away with her tears.

Tom sat back down on the couch, very still now. He didn't do well with a weeping woman and immediately felt guilty, transported back to his childhood. Bernice knew the story: His dad always made his mother cry. He often came home, finding his mom behind the stove cooking supper while wiping her eyes with a hanky, all soaked through with tears. Invariably, he would try to console his mom asking what was wrong, but then she denied she'd been crying, in spite of the obvious. Tom carried his hate for his dad into adulthood. Ever since knowing this, she tried to not cry, but this time she was unable to put her own needs aside.

Bernice wept with her hands before her face, quietly, until she felt Tom sit down beside her on the couch and his arm around her, gently shushing her. "There, there. It'll be alright. Don't cry Bernie, oh, Bernie, I still love you, just with a different kind of love. I'll never leave you. Come dry your tears. Let's go at this in a constructive way. Now the cat is out of the bag, we can be honest. I'm sure that it'll all work itself out in the end."

In spite of her distrust, Bernice stopped crying, got up and walked towards the bathroom, got a tissue and blew her nose. She splashed cold water on her face and took the towel, softly patting her cheeks, leaving some moisture on her eyes, careful not to rub them, believing that rubbing one's eyes would stretch the sensitive tissue, causing wrinkles. She'd read that somewhere. Her hands trembled, her nausea stuck in her stomach, and a heavy feeling settled in her chest. She took a few deep breaths in and slowly out again and then returned to Tom, still quietly sitting on the couch.

She dropped down on the couch across from him. She felt drunk. She remembered him assuring her he didn't want to abandon her and the children. Feeling stretched beyond her capacity, she looked at him, studying his face while he stared out the window, deep in thought. His features were still handsome, graying at the temples and tanned from playing golf three times a week. His hair was thinning on top, but with his new brush cut, the baldness seemed less obvious. It made him actually look quite macho.

Her heart ached, knowing he wasn't in love with her anymore. Tears again collected in her eyes, threatening to overflow. "What are we going to do now?" she asked softly. Speaking was better than thinking; then she could somehow swallow her tears.

"I'm not sure. I think the earlier notion I mentioned about a schedule with the kids' sport clubs is a good idea. Then we know ahead of time where we're supposed to be. I know we sort of did that before, but I admit I took advantage of you. From now on I'll see to it being there for the children when I need to be." Tom seemed satisfied with his own speech and stood up, turned to Bernice with eyes raised, waiting for her response, which wasn't what he expected.

Bernice's voice had recovered and she spoke businesslike, almost stern, matching his demeanor. "Are you planning on seeing her again? I need to know. I also want to know what you see in her. What's she got that you're missing in me?"

"Bernice, that's a very personal question. I'm not sure that I can answer that. Marla and I just hit it off. She is beautiful and young, and she seems to think I'm great. I don't get that from you anymore – that you think I'm great, I mean."

Bernice fought to keep in control, shocked by Tom's answer. "Of course I'm older now, compared to her, and you're flattered by her attention. That's just lust. But what about our relationship? Isn't there anything we could do, anything you want me to change? We should see a counsellor. I don't want to give up on our marriage."

"Well, what can I say? You seem bored with me; the last years you've been all about the kids. That was apparently enough for you, but it wasn't for me. Let's just see how things go for a while and let's not make any hasty decisions. What do you say?"

After so much disclosure of his innermost feelings, Tom seemed to withdraw into himself again, as if he'd startled himself by speaking out and she saw he was about to leave the room. She realized he had voiced more criticism now than he had shared during their whole marriage; he must be just as stressed as she was. Reluctantly she responded.

"Okay, then; I can wait a while and let's see what you will do. I'll give you time to sort out what you want. Just one thing: I don't want you to bring that woman here, or take her with you when you do things with the kids. Keep her to yourself, please. Can you at least do that?" She got up and took a few steps closer to Tom, stopped right in front of him; she could feel his breath on her cheek.

He looked down – a head taller than her – and almost automatically kissed her on her forehead. Her instinct was right – he was without passion – and starting that habit should have alerted her, years back.

"I promise."

Exhausted, they retreated to their own spaces, left alone with their own truths, but not necessarily the same truths: Tom to the den and his computer, Bernice to her bedroom.

The next morning, Bernice's heart still hurt, and the pain of Tom's betrayal recirculated in every breath she took as she got dressed and went to the kitchen. With her steady nature and her resolve to keep him attached to her family, she was able to suppress much of the pain. She began to understand that she would have more time to herself – if Tom stuck to his promise with the schedule in place. Maybe she should return to yoga and medication classes, something just for her.

Hey, that was strange: Tom left her a note on the counter, in a sealed envelope. Premonition caused her neck hairs to stand up. With the envelope in her hand, she took the few steps back to her bedroom in a hurry, closing the door behind her. She ripped the envelope open with a trembling fingertip. She read:

"*Bernice,*

I feel so bad about what happened. I did not mean to hurt you. I apologize and I am begging you for forgiveness. I have made some decisions that I wanted to let you know right away. I am going to look for a space of my own and will not sleep at home for a while. I need to make up my mind without you. I want to give my relationship with Marla a chance. Please, understand that I have to do this for me. I will do everything for the kids, as I said I would, and the schedule on the fridge is what I will follow. I will not desert the children and I will be their parent to the best of my abilities. Please, forgive me. Tom."

Bernice sat down on the bed, Tom's letter next to her. Her thoughts had slowed down; one thought trickled in, then another. How could she be so stupid? Last night she thought they might have it out and then make up, maybe even have make-up sex. She didn't read him right at all; she'd been all wrong. He was a stranger to her; she never knew him at all. Her marriage was a farce, her life all pretense.

Like a robot, she returned to her pattern of coping she had developed after Daniel's arrival: Focus on the children. What was she going to tell them today? The boys would arrive first – very soon – and Shayla would be last. The boys would be easy; they would just accept whatever their mom told them. Abby would ask a bit more, but still, she would go with the flow. Shayla, with little trust in adults, would be hardest to tell about this family disaster.

Thinking about Shayla brought a notion to the foreground, buried in her subconscious until now: Something was going on with Shayla. She seemed so distant this last week, as if she was shutting her out. Preoccupied with Tom, she had glossed over Shayla's unusual need to be out of the house so often. She wondered what that could be all about.

CHAPTER 16

Arranged in pairs – Shayla with Eric, Jake and Ellen, and Kyle with Anita – the friends took over Ellen's living room, making themselves comfortable on the couches and the floor, the guys with bottles of Coors in their hands and the girls with coolers, with more beers and coolers keeping cool in the fridge. Ellen had supplied chips and dip and other snacks, displayed on the coffee table, next to of Eric's vaporizer; he also had provided the pot. Loud music from the stereo system interfered with conversation, but the couples weren't much into talking – too busy making out.

Ellen got up and opened a window. "It's too smoky in here, my mom will notice," she yelled. Nobody replied.

Shayla looked into Eric's eyes – the whites just as red as hers – and she smiled; he pulled her face towards him and spoke into her ear: "Let's go to the basement." He pulled her up by her hand while getting up from the floor in one smooth movement, Shayla following willingly. Hanging on to him with both her arms around his neck, as if she was drowning and he was to save her, they walked the few treads and almost tumbled down the stairs together.

In the basement guest room, they lost their balance willingly and fell over on top of the double bed entangled in an embrace: Shayla's leg behind his torso, with her other leg over his waist. Eric untangled himself while tugging at her dress, trying to get it over her head. She helped him, then threw the fancy dress on the floor and bent her torso, so he could easier get at her bra closure, which left her in her panties. He pushed Shayla back on the bed and quickly undressed while Shayla was watching him. A floor lamp in one corner of the room spread a creamy light onto the ceiling.

Shayla's senses absorbed it all: The soft bed, the sheets cool, and their bodies together radiating heat to the dangerous level of a potential spontaneous combustion, which led to a conscious thought at the last minute. Shayla remembered: "The condom!" Eric grabbed his jeans from the floor, fishing the lifesaver from his jeans pocket. The actual moment of "it" was over before she realized it. The earth didn't move and she didn't feel ecstasy, just a sharp, brief cramp when Eric pushed his way into her. It was all rather disappointing.

Eric looked very happy and kissed her all over. "Thank you, thank you," he murmured in her ear. She didn't know what to reply, but felt a little better by his response. His face rested on her shoulder and he seemed to fade away. She was thinking about what she would tell her friends about this, when she felt something sticky between her legs and thought she'd better get up before the sheets were ruined. She grabbed the box with tissues from the bedside table reaching over him and noticed he had fallen asleep.

Carefully she slipped away from him, making sure to let his face gently land on the pillow. She freshened herself up in the basement bathroom and noticed some bleeding, as if she just started her period; she found some feminine hygiene products in the cabinet and got dressed. The music was blaring upstairs, but she didn't want to join the others, not yet. She sat down beside the bed on the floor, watching

Eric's face while he slept. He looked very young and sweet. Could she trust him or would he leave her for another girl?

She compared herself with Ellen – so much prettier and a lot less shy, but she would never cheat on Eric like Ellen did with Jake; but then again, Jake didn't stick to Ellen only either. She didn't want that for her and Eric. She was his girlfriend now, through thick and thin, whatever may happen, and she was going to tell her mom about it.

CHAPTER 17

Bernice had her first cup of coffee this Sunday morning in her bedroom and not in the kitchen as usual. She hadn't slept much; her head felt like a vacuum-packed bag with cotton balls; she was unable to think – didn't want to think. How the hell had she arrived at this point in life with four kids, a taxing job, and a deserting husband?

At the start of her adult life, she had chosen so well, had stuck to her plan to marry only after graduation from university, and finally agreed to marry her high school sweetheart. Their marriage was known among their friends as a model marriage. All was good for many years. When did things get off the rails? More specifically, what was the moment that Tom lost interest in her? She tried to think back, but nothing came to mind.

Why did she have so much trouble with expressing anger? She tried to give her anger a voice and said out loud what came up spontaneously; the only words that surfaced were derogative names, which wasn't like her. Yesterday she had cleaned house, keeping her anger in; after that she investigated. She went through Tom's office, trying to find any scraps of paper, any indication of what went wrong. She went into his files and looked at the family paperwork he usually took care of: the bills, the mortgage, and the investments.

In front of her on the bedroom floor sat a stack of papers that looked like bank statements of investments and RRSPs, she had separated from the rest. She did not really know what it all meant, but realized that Tom had been accumulating a nest egg. The thought that a divorce was becoming a reality in her life flashed up after she raided the file cabinet, but she didn't really want to think about that. Then what was she going to do with those papers? Maybe she should copy them, just in case. She wanted to ask Tom about it, call him, but decided she didn't want to face the humiliation that she might get Marla when she called him. What did he see in that child? She was just a few years older than Shayla, for god sakes.

The boys were up; she heard their voices coming from the family room, where they were watching the weekend cartoons. After the big reveal, she had missed the kids that night; nevertheless, she was grateful they had not seen her at her worst. When the boys came home on Saturday, she hadn't been much of a parent and let them have more video game time than ever before. At least she had Kate and Beth's support, no strangers to turmoil in a relationship; they had their separations and bad patches.

Bernice suddenly realized she was supposed to pick up Abby from her friend's house in an hour. Shayla should be coming home from her stay over at Ellen's later in the morning. She wondered how that had been, and whether Ellen's mom had come home late again. She made a heroic effort to reign in her thoughts, put on a happy face and left the bedroom. She shouted down the stairs: "Hey, Daniel, Jon, are you hungry? What would you like for breakfast?"

The boys came running up the stairs and joined Bernice in the kitchen, eager to get their usual Sunday breakfast. Daniel, always quicker than Jonathan, said, "I want waffles, can you make waffles, mom?"

"No, I want scrambled eggs, it's my turn to say," Daniel replied.

Bernice felt not up to the battle and replied: "How about I make both?"

After breakfast she picked up Abby, and Shayla came home some-time later in the morning. Bernice got through the day somehow, spending more time than usual in her bedroom, grateful that the chil-dren had themselves a quiet day after their late night stay-overs. She noticed that nobody asked about their dad.

When all were seated at the dinner table that evening, Bernice told the children the news. "Daddy is away for a while. Daniel and Jonathan, don't worry; he'll pick you guys up as usual for the practices and games. We'll have our family celebrations together as usual and when Dad is needed, we can call him anytime, and he'll come to help out."

The boys seemed oblivious to the news. As long as their dad was present for their important stuff, they would be okay – already used to his absence – and no different from the usual. Abby was the first one to catch on to the reality. "Why didn't Dad sleep here, Mom? Did you have a fight?"

"Well, yes, sort of, but it has nothing to do you with you guys; that's between me and Dad. Nothing for you guys to worry about."

Shayla usually was the anxious one, and instantly reactive. Not this time; she seemed withdrawn, indifferent even, and not what Bernice would expect when she eventually commented: "Oh, well, he'll be okay. I'm sure it will be solved soon between you. Can I stay tomorrow for supper at Anita's? I want to work with her on a project for socials. I'll be home by eight or nine."

Bernice scanned Shayla's face for any signs of anxiety – there weren't any. "Okay. That's fine." She wanted to expand, but stopped herself.

———

The following morning, everything went as usual at the Harrison home: The kids were off to school and Bernice went off to work. Her day was erratic and so were her thoughts; in spite of her efforts to focus, her mind had a will of its own and repeated the same thoughts like a melody, an earworm stuck in her head: He left me, he said he wouldn't, why did he leave me?

The usual range of clients passed through her day: A young mother in tears who pleaded with her to have her child returned in spite of having a dirty drug screen. A father accused Bernice of choosing the side of his ex. A ten-year-old youth was reluctant to talk to her – understandably and obviously loyal to his mom. Bernice went through the motions, waiting for the day to end. It was now 3:30 p.m.; another hour to go.

She got up from her desk and walked to the kitchen to put the kettle on for a cup of tea, waited around until it boiled and walked with her cup cum tea bag, back towards her office. She heard the phone rang in her office from the corridor, quickened her step and caught the call just in time.

A youngish voice asked: "Hello, Officer Ellen Johnston here from the local police detachment; is this Bernice Harrison?"

Bernice was waiting for a call back on a youth who went AWOL from his foster home. "Yes, speaking. How can I help you?"

"Bernice, I would like you to come to the station, if at all possible. I need you to I.D. a young lady that we have here for questioning. She says you are her mother."

Bernice thought she had not heard correctly. "Excuse me, officer, did you say a young lady? What's her name?"

"She says her name is Shayla Harrison, age seventeen."

"Oh, no! Is she all right? Yes, that is my daughter. Did something happen to her?" Bernice's brain refused to get it.

The cop replied with a careful, slowly spoken explanation: "If you mean if she is hurt, no, ma'am, she's not hurt. We have her here for an interview regarding an alleged shoplifting incident. She was brought in about an hour ago and we would like to question her, but she's under-age, so we're obliged to try to reach the guardian first. That would be you, is that correct?"

Her mind slowly opened up for the word 'shoplifting'. "Yes, that's correct. I can be there in about fifteen."

"Okay, then, Ms. Harrison, we'll wait for you. Ask for Officer Johnston at the counter and the clerk will take you to the interview room."

Bernice's heart was pounding. She grabbed her purse and rushed to the exit, not signing out, not thinking about anything else, but Shayla. Oh, Shayla, my girl, what were you thinking? Don't we have enough trouble already? Ten minutes later, the reception clerk led Bernice into the interview room she'd seen before, when picking-up, or bringing in foster children for an interview – a bare room with a steel table and benches on either side screwed onto the floor.

Within seconds of Bernice's arrival, Shayla and the constable entered, and the constable introduced herself. Shayla didn't look at her mother and sat down next to Bernice, her eyes downcast, staring at the tabletop. The officer was a young woman who sat down across from her; to Bernice she didn't look much older than her daughter. Bernice, sitting close to Shayla, couldn't help, but wish she'd be here for one of her other foster children, and not for her own daughter.

"Well, what do we have here," Constable Johnston started. She looked at Bernice. "Shayla and I met a couple of hours ago at the mall. I'm assigned to work with youth."

Then she turned to Shayla: "Shayla, you were picked up by us after a call from a department store that you were observed taking some clothing into the dressing room and apparently, you didn't come out with the same number of items. The clerks passed on the info to security; on you trying to leave the store, the loss prevention staff interrupted your departure and detained you, Shayla, in the store office, from where he called the police. He apparently had met you before in similar circumstances. You then admitted that you were wearing some of the clothing that you hadn't paid for. So here we are."

Shayla kept her gaze down staring down at the table and didn't reply. Bernice spoke up. "Is this true, Shayla? Look at me, please."

"Yes," Shayla answered quietly, not looking up. Bernice helplessly looked at the officer, with her hands spread wide before her. "I just don't know why she'd do that. She has no lack of anything." She then clasped her hands together, as if praying.

"Yes, ma'am, there's often no reason for it that we adults can see, but it happens all the time. Tell me, Shayla, is there anything that worries you? School? Boyfriend? Parents fighting? Are others picking on you at school, or cyber-bullying you on the Internet?" Bernice held her breath, awaiting Shayla's answer.

Shayla shrugged her shoulders and slowly replied, "No."

Bernice exhaled and asked the officer "What will happen now; will you let her go home with me?"

"Not so quickly, Ms. Harrison. Shayla, have you done this before? And if so, how many times?"

"Only once before and I'll never do it again. I promise. I don't know why I did that; it's so stupid. The jeans were just so cool, but too expensive. I had to have them. I will pay for it; I have money." Subdued, she looked at the officer, still avoiding Bernice's eyes.

"Yes, that's what we hear more often. Sometimes we girls don't even know that we are not feeling that good about ourselves and then we do things on impulse that we'd never do, if we had thought about it for a second. Do you get along with your parents, Shayla?"

Bernice's body stiffened for the answer. Shayla was still not looking at her mom, but was looking square at the officer, her voice a bit more assertive, almost a tad defiant.

"Yes, we get along okay. Like, my mom is busy with her work and all. She's my adoptive mom. I get along fine with my dad. He's busy too. Like, I don't get to see him much. I have another dad, my birth dad, but I haven't seen him in about ten years or so, like, since when I was little."

"It that right? Is that something that you wished would happen?" The officer seems to show more interest in the interview, perked up her demeanor by straightening her spine and rolling her shoulders back, now paying close attention to Shayla.

"Yes, I think I would like to see him, like, he's my birth dad, like, he was doing drugs, so….and maybe he still is….so, I can't see him, my parents said."

"Ms. Harrison, care to comment?"

Officer Ellen Johnston looked at Bernice with raised eyebrows, fixing her steady gaze on her. Bernice stayed quiet for some minutes. Finally, she replied: "Yes, it's a bit of a problem that has caused some stress in the family. But we're dealing with it and we're working on a first meeting in the future, after I checked him out."

From her peripheral view, she became aware that Shayla looked at her for the first time, and she quickly glanced at her daughter. With great defiance in her eyes, Shayla glared back at her with an intensity of resentment that Bernice had never felt before from her daughter.

The officer turned to Shyla. "Well, that's maybe something you could discuss further at home with your parents. You'll have to come to court, Shayla, because you committed a criminal act and have to explain yourself to the judge under the Young Persons' Act. The store is pressuring for charges; it's up to the crown prosecutor and the judge whether anything further will happen. Be at court at 9 a.m. on Wednesday; you must report to Room 101 on the main floor. Then you'll get assigned a date for a first court appearance. Do you have any questions?"

Shayla's lip trembled when she asked: "Do I have to go to jail?"

"Well, I can't say, of course; we never know what will come of it, but if the judge has in mind that you are a first offender and this is a minor charge, you might get community service or probation. So, of course, the offence cannot happen again. I hope you know that now, do you?"

"I know," Shayla replied softly, head bent, tears rolling down her cheeks, hastily wiped away, with her long hair obscuring most of her face. Bernice wanted to touch her, put an arm around her shoulders, but restrained herself.

Twenty minutes after she first got there, Bernice walked with Shayla to her car. She asked as gently as possible: "Are you all right, sweetheart?"

Suddenly she felt Shayla's arms around her. She hugged her back and held Shayla tightly against her, until Shayla disentangled herself. "Oh, mom, I'm so sorry, so sorry. I am so stupid to do that to you. Like, I didn't know about you and dad having troubles." She gently told Shayla to get in the car; once inside, she kept talking.

"It's okay, sweetheart; you really couldn't know and it's not of your concern, no need to worry about that; it's for me and dad to deal with. I'm sorry, too. I didn't know you had a much harder time than it looked on the surface, I mean with not getting to see Gabriel; I'm sorry it got postponed. You know what? We'll work on that in the next while. I could see whether I can meet with him to do my own checking up. That's the very least I can do. Is that okay?"

"Oh, yes, that's great. I hope he's clean, right? Wouldn't it be great, if I had two dads? Are you going to tell dad about the shoplifting?"

"Of course; Dad needs to know. It's not good to have secrets among family members. You know he'll be disappointed, and he might get angry at you, at first. But he will support you and do whatever is best for you. He loves you; you do know that, don't you? Maybe he can go to court with you; what do you think?"

"I know. I hope he won't be very mad; like, he gets so cold. I'm afraid he won't love me anymore when he hears what I've done. Will you be there the whole time, mom?"

"Sure." Bernice was silent for a few minutes, then she continued: "You will be grounded, Shayla, I'll tell you that much. Your dad and

I will discuss it and decide together for how long, but of course there must be consequences for stealing."

She started the car and drove away, deep in thought, wondering what the future would bring. Could her daughter escape the fate of so many foster children, a life of insecurity, of failed relationships and borderline criminality? Was she wrong all along to adopt Shayla and Abby and push Tom into it? Now that she was losing him and raising four children on her own as her new future, she wasn't so sure anymore. Her resolve and energy almost audibly escape from her when she let out a deep sigh, like air burbling from a balloon when letting go of its mouthpiece.

CHAPTER 18

Shoplifting had become quite a habit by then, but she couldn't admit the full extent to anybody; she would be grounded and her life ruined. Her wardrobe contained several new pieces that she never even showed to her mom; she'll keep that secret to herself. Now that she was caught, it had to be over. Riding at home with her mom, Shayla contemplated the fall-out from her capture by that nasty store detective.

What would be the right moment for a confession about Eric? She quickly glanced at her mother's face. Maybe not now while she's driving. She remembered her mom's talk with her about having sex for the first time, and about birth control; she hoped her mom would understand, now it actually had happened. At the police station, talking about wanting to see Gabriel, she'd been curious what her mom really thought. She had glanced sideways again, but saw nothing on her mom's face. How do adults do that, put on that stone face? Now she was paying attention to the heavy traffic.

The police knew her now as a criminal; that wasn't good. Did she have the gene for being bad? Was she a criminal like Nora? Or weak like Gabriel? Could she even make it in the world, or was she emotionally crippled? Why did she even steal those things? It didn't seem worth it now.

Ellen and Anita might tell her she's all right, but what if they wouldn't like her anymore, after she tells them the truth? They might be mad at her about not telling – they shared all their secrets. Ellen's mom was pretty cool and easy-going and broke the rules herself – but she probably would say that stealing isn't cool. Everybody would think her a loser for having to steal clothes, even missus G, especially if they knew her other reason – stealing to impress a boyfriend.

She looked at her mom again, her face was still frozen. Was she mad? Even so, that wouldn't be the end of the world; she usually got over tiffs quickly, but what would matter was the loss in trust, of her belief in her, when she found out she had lied so much. That would be the very worst. Her mom always believed in her, but when the last person that loved her gave up on her, she'd be – worthless. She wanted to crawl into bed and never come out to face the world.

They arrived home. She felt the house was too large, too dark. It looked deserted; an eerie light fell through the windows. She jumped when her mom spoke: "Would you turn on some lights, please? I bet we'll be getting a storm. Just go to your room, honey; try to do some homework. I'm getting the kids from the sitter; I'm late already. We'll talk later, after I speak with your dad."

In her room, Shayla sat down on her bed and opened the drawer of her bedside table. Slowly she took a Bic shaver from it, pushed up a sleeve and let the blade glide laterally along her underarm into the soft part. A thin line of red appeared, but no blood escaped to roll down her arm. The line's end joined the other crusty brown stripes and white scar lines from previous cuts. She looked at it, feeling a bit better. She quickly pulled her sleeve over the cut and then the feeling came back into her, a sharp sort of pain, not intense, but more of a nagging presence.

———————

The next morning, Shayla sat down at the breakfast table and took a deep breath. While she grabbed the cereal box, and before she could change her mind, she blurted out, "Mom, I have to tell you something, can we talk now?"

"Sure, sweetheart. What's up?"

"Last weekend when I stayed over at Ellen's, I had sex with Eric. Are you mad?"

Bernice dropped the cup of coffee she had just poured, suddenly unable to hold on to it. The cup clattered in the sink, breaking off its handle. "What did you say, did I hear that right? You had sex? At Ellen's place?"

"I'd thought I'd better tell you, because I feel bad about keeping secrets from you. Are you disappointed in me?"

"Oh my, I'll have think about that. Right away I have a lot of questions. In any case, I'm not sure that this is the right time to talk about it. We have to talk yet about the thefts and dad and I haven't finished talking yet about that. The boys and Abby will be down for breakfast any minute now and then we'll have to get on our way. How about tonight after school; can we talk then? Dad will be with the boys at soccer practice and only Abby will be home. I'll try to get home early from work."

Her mom threw the broken cup in the garbage, got a new cup and poured another coffee. Standing by the sink she carefully sipped her hot liquid, with a facial expression that looked like she was deep in thought. Shayla anxiously eyed her mom, looking for any signs on her face – she didn't see any. She pressed on.

"Okay, but are you mad, mom?"

"I'm surprised and somewhat shocked that my girl has grown up that quickly, but, no, I'm not mad, just glad that you told me. I agree with you, it's not good to have secrets, so thank you for sharing that important news. Just one question: Did you use anything, a condom?"

"Yes, mom. Eric is a responsible guy."

"Good, then we'll talk more tonight. Let me give you a hug." Her mom walked around the breakfast bar and gave her a quick hug and a kiss on her forehead, reaching up on tippy-toes, as they were just about the same size, she a tad taller than her mom. To her surprise, Bernice didn't say anything more.

Shayla sat down and gobbled up her cereal. She put her empty bowl in the dishwasher, rummaged through the shelves of the fridge to get her things for lunch and then left the kitchen, looking back one more time at her mom for reassurance. Her mom smiled at her when she left the kitchen.

CHAPTER 19

After Shayla's revelation, Bernice had to bite her lips and tongue to withhold the questions that were making her blood boil, but she didn't ask: Where was Ellen's mom that this could happen? Was there alcohol involved again, or maybe even drugs? Was Ellen's mom even at her home at all that night? What kind of a mother was Ellen's mom? She must be one of those mothers who would rather be buddies with their children, and avoid at all costs the disciplinarian role. Sure, that's nice; Bernice would love to be that friend to her girl, but she had too much sense of responsibility, and simply had no other choice, aware of the consequences of spineless parenting.

She had seen it many times before, so *she* had taken on the responsible adult role for her children. Bernice then realized things weren't going that well for her family. Maybe she should have been more playful and less of a drag. She never had any doubts before, but now she wasn't so sure; maybe she wasn't always right. Tom was leaving her for this airhead, Shayla was caught shoplifting, and on top of that, she could become pregnant in the near future, or run to her biological relatives, and she herself was overworked and anxious.

She had to admit she wasn't deriving the same pleasure from work she once experienced. She hardly got to see her friends. Now that her family was falling apart, couples would become uncomfortable with a single woman in their company; soon she might not have any friends left. That's the way it usually went – the women got fearful of losing their husband to a free woman.

As a single mother with four kids, the end of her bright future was looming. She wouldn't be an attractive partner to anybody, not even to the most generous and kind man. It wasn't what she set out for when she and Tom adopted Shayla and Abby.

Standing in the middle of the kitchen, Bernice seemed frozen. She stared into the distance through the kitchen window, holding a colourful, nylon lunch bag in her hands. What had happened? Had she been too strident and pushy, ignoring to press harder for Tom's input and his opinions to her own detriment? Did she give Shayla too little of her time and attention? Had she been too focused on setting boundaries and being the heavy? Bernice let out a deep sigh and then opened the fridge and packed her lunch in the bag. Life is just too difficult.

Jonathan noisily rolled into the kitchen together with Daniel. "Mom, is Dad coming to pick us up from school today?"

"Yes, my boys. Be sure to be standing at the entrance, so Dad can see you and you won't be late for practice. Have you decided where you want to go for your supper with Dad afterwards? Let me see your soccer bag. Have you put clean socks in there for after practice?"

"Yes, we want to go to Taco Time, we haven't been there in a while."

"Good, does Dad know?"

"Yes, we told him last night when he called."

"Be careful that you don't put too much of the hot sauce on them, as last time you didn't want to eat your tacos." She checked the boys' bags and helped them pack their lunches, then poured each a glass of juice, while they ate their breakfast: Choco Puffs. They have been rather indulgent with the boys. "Pick your battles," Tom would say when she objected to the boys' choice of cereals while shopping. "At least they have no problems with eating and they'll work off the extra energy."

Abby entered the kitchen; she liked to wait until her brothers were almost gone, craving the time and extra attention. "Mom, will you take me for supper to the Wrap Zone? I haven't been there in such a long time. It's not fair that the boys get to go out for fast food all the time when Dad takes them."

"Sure, honey. Did you practice your piece long enough for your teacher yesterday? I timed you and you played only 20 instead of 30 minutes. It's a good thing I can hear the piano from anywhere in the house."

"Mom, don't bug me. I was tired last night. I'll play extra-long tonight, okay?"

Then they were off to school and work.

In the evening, Bernice sat in her bedroom on the love seat. When she heard Shayla come up the stairs, she called out through the open bedroom door. "Shayla, I'm here, want to join me?"

Shayla came in, still dressed in her exercise outfit from ballet class.

"We were planning on talking, but Abby wanted to have some time, sorry about that."

"That's okay, mom. Can we keep it short? I'm tired, the class was intense and I talked to my instructor about Eric after. She understands and was very nice to me."

"Sure. I'm happy to keep our talk short, if that's what you want. I am here for you, so it's up to you, really, how long we talk. By the way, have you heard from Anna yet? I almost forgot about her, but I still want to speak with Gabriel first; you were going to ask her to give me his phone number or his email address, remember?"

"Yes, right! As if I would forget, after all that trouble the first time! I'll copy you her last email, so you'll have her address. You know, I already told Anna about you and Dad not letting me get in touch with Gabriel. You can tell her yourself that you changed your mind, right?" Shayla looked with curiosity at her mom to see what she would do with that situation, where she had to backtrack on an earlier decision. But Bernice didn't bat an eye and replied easily.

"Okay, that sounds good. I'll email her in a minute for Gabriel's information. Now you want to tell me how your stay over at Ellen's went?"

Bernice heard an abbreviated version of what had passed last Saturday at Ellen's and how Shayla 'gave herself to Eric', as she put it. Shayla's face shone at the recall and she blushed deeply when she came to the words, looking down at her fingers, nervously picking at her nails while exclaiming "omigod" often. After she got it all out, she shyly looked up at Bernice to see what her mom's face would say.

Bernice couldn't help but getting mildly irritated by the naiveté displayed by her daughter, but would not crush her daughter's happiness. She knew life would do that all on its own soon enough. "I'm happy for you that you found a sweet boy who's considerate. You were sure you were ready to have sex then? He did not put any pressure on you?"

"No, not at all. I wanted it too, mom."

"Well, I guess you have the age and yes, the circumstances were right, in a bed. I'm glad that you had a good first experience. If I were in Ellen's mom's shoes, I probably wouldn't have allowed it, I mean for guys to stay at an unsupervised party, but that's water under the bridge now. I do have some questions. Did you guys have any alcohol in the house? It's still illegal at your age and many kids get into car crashes."

"Why are you asking? We were not drunk, or anything, if you think that," Shayla replied with a sudden defiance in her voice.

Bernice recognized the signs. She warned herself to tread carefully and took a slow and deep breath, forcing herself to stay calm. She carefully continued. "Well, sweetheart, it does matter. Alcohol takes away inhibitions, so your impulses are set free. The other biochemical reaction to alcohol is a depressed metabolism, so a person's thinking capacity and general functioning, such as your ability to drive and react, goes down. That's why decisions made under alcohol are often poor ones that might have been different had the person been sober. I don't want you to make the wrong decisions and later be sorry that you did what you did."

She mustered up the courage and willpower to keep her feelings under control, but her heart pounded and she folded her hands in a tight grip to prevent them from shaking, as if she was praying. She wanted to scream and hurl into her daughter's face that both her parents were addicts and ask what made her think she could do any of that.

"Mom, I wanted it and I was not drunk." Shayla pulled back into her seat, folding her arms over her chest.

"How about Eric, was he drinking?"

Bernice didn't know him; for all she knew he might be her daughter's predator, a boy with too much testosterone, out for one thing only.

153

He would surely break her daughter's heart, just like Tom had broken hers.

"Mom, stop it. He just had a few beers, that's all. You are social-working me. If you're going to interrogate me, I'm outta here." Shayla got up from her seat.

"Please, sit down, Shayla. I know it's not easy to talk about these things, but it's important we do."

Shayla sat down at the edge of her chair, her head tilted backwards a tad, and her chin jutting out, but still wanting to please her mom.

"I also would like to know who bought the alcohol and whether Ellen's mom knew about it," Bernice continued stubbornly.

"Mom, stop it! What does that matter? Like, you don't have to know everything! Why do you care? I am seventeen!"

Bernice couldn't help herself; the social worker in her took over, but as a mother, she avoided getting to the heart of the matter and couldn't broach with Shayla her familial vulnerabilities. "Well, Shayla, I'll tell you why it matters: Ellen's mother is the adult and should supervise her daughter and make sure no accidents could happen. You know as well as I do, that drunk driving by underage youths takes many lives. If something happened at her place, Ellen's mom would be responsible and in that case, any parent whose kid was at her house, including me, could sue her."

"Oh Mom, please! Stop It!"

"I'm worried about you. From now on I won't allow you to stay overnight anymore at Ellen's and I want to speak with her mother about this. Well, was she there on Saturday night, or wasn't she?"

Shayla was already marching out of the room, stomping her feet, head held up high while calling out over her shoulder, "Why don't you ask her yourself? Right? You are ruining my life! I hate you."

CHAPTER 20

Shayla was worried. Everything she feared had come true. Her friends hated her; she wasn't invited anymore to their get-togethers, because she'd ratted them out. It was Saturday and she sat in her room, grounded, nowhere to go, nobody to see, nobody to text or call. Her life was ruined. Ellen told her outright how stupid she had been.

"Why did you have to blabber to your mom about us? Like, it's none of her business. Could you not just keep your mouth shut? And then, listen to this, she said to my mom you stole and got caught? How stupid is that? What did you steal anyway? My mom laughed and said you're not smart enough to stay out of trouble. You're a loser. Like, if Eric hears you're grounded and why, he'll also think you're an idiot. Like, he was asking if you were coming out to my place again and I told him not likely."

Eric, yes, him. At least her mom let her keep her cell phone. She had texted him that she was grounded. He texted back that it didn't matter, he'd wait for her, although she wasn't sure she could believe him. If Anita and Ellen talked to him before she did, they would tell him all about her stupidity.

Her room was getting darker and it was getting late. Her life sucked. She wanted to die. She paced from one side of the room to the other, thinking up ways to escape. She sat down on the bed, opened her laptop and started e-mailing her sister Anna: Have you given my mom your dad's email address yet? She waited. She was getting lucky; Anna was online.

Anna wrote back that she had and asked how she was, and she hadn't heard from her in a while. "I'm in trouble," she wrote back. "I'm grounded because I had a party at my friends' place and like, we got caught having liquor. And I got caught shoplifting too. Have you ever done that? I didn't want to tell you that before, as maybe you'd also think me a loser, like my friends did."

She anxiously waited for the answer that came within seconds. "Oh shit, yes. Who hasn't? I never got caught. Did it with my mom; she taught me how to do it. When my mom really got into trouble and when my brother and I went into foster care, I stopped doing it."

Shayla couldn't believe her eyes when she read the lines, and admired Anna's ease of putting down that damaging sentence, so readily and openly; it baffled her. Shayla wanted to know if she and Abby were already born, back then. "No, I heard you got born when I was about ten, or so, like, when mom got a new man. She had several boyfriends – I never knew who she was with – but I hardly saw her back then anyway. I was in a foster home and she didn't do visiting."

"That sounds like her; she did that with us too." Shayla replied, and had another important question, aware that the mother lode was now exposed to her. She asked about Nora's trouble, whether it was about drugs.

Anna wrote: "I don't know for sure what drugs, but she was busted several times for trafficking and I wasn't allowed to see her anymore after that. That's how I knew, because my social worker told me and said it would be bad for me to see her without somebody supervising, and my mom wanted nobody supervising."

Fascinated, a stream of questions popped into her head, becoming aware that she might get to know a truth existed she couldn't even have imagined. She asked who her dad was and whether he also was a dealer, how Anna knew him and how he is doing now. Her fingers typed away at a frantic pace and she didn't bother correcting spelling mistakes.

And the answer: "No, he's not related to me. Gabriel told me he was also into drugs, not sure if he was a dealer, you'd have to ask him yourself one day. He's just a good guy now. After he got clean, he was looking for family, so he found me, because I have my mother's name. Got to go, sweetie. My kids need to go to bed. TTYL. Love you."

———————

Shayla had no idea what to do next. She fell back on her bed and stared at the ceiling while thoughts tumbled around in her head: Maybe Nora taught her also how to shoplift when she was little and she just didn't remember. If her dad wouldn't come back and gets a divorce, she'll still have another dad who wants her – Gabriel.

Maybe she was not doomed, because Anna became normal, at least she sounds normal, with children that were not taken from her. Compared to Anna, she even had a better life, as her social worker became her mom. She has to believe Bernice wanted what's best for her, that she loved her, and she couldn't imagine not having her mom in her life. Was she going to have others in her life that loved her? Would she see Eric again? Gabriel? She wanted to see Anna and talk more, know what she knows. Maybe Anna could tell her more about that empty feeling inside her, the sadness, the feeling that nobody loved her, and how to get rid of it.

Slowly she pushed herself to sitting and stared out the window of her bedroom without seeing. Maybe it would be best to talk to her mom and ask her about Gabriel. She realized she would need her mom, if anything was going to happen about meeting Gabriel. She really, really needed her now. Maybe it was good that she found out things the hard way, as now she understood more about herself, and about what happened to her. Maybe it's true what her mom always said: Things need to get worse before they get better.

CHAPTER 21

Bernice and Kate strolled down Main Street on their way to the car from the movie theatre, chatting and gesticulating, grabbing each other's arm occasionally to emphasize a point. Shayla was at home looking after the little ones – a lucky side effect of grounding. Bernice had decided to take advantage of this opportunity to have some fun and see the movie The Help, a popular and widely discussed film, in a movie review characterized as a chick flick of some substance, but still lightweight entertainment.

Suddenly, her heart seemed to stop beating for a few seconds, then started up again in an escalated rhythm. Her ears started buzzing and she felt as if she was going to faint. She grabbed onto Kate's arm tightly and stammered: "Look across the road."

Kate looked in the direction of Bernice's stare. She saw two people leaving a Japanese restaurant across the street, clearly a couple, arms around each other, chatting and very much into each other, unaware of anyone else.

"Oh my God, that's Tom. I'm so sorry. Bernice, you alright? Your face is as white as a brand new terry towel." And her body as pliable: Bernice's knees buckled underneath her. Kate firmly grabbed Bernice around her back at the waist with one arm, took her hand leading her into the other direction, away from the scene across the road.

"You need a drink. Let's just go into The Keg here and get a drink." Without speaking they entered the bar and sat down. Kate ordered two shots of tequila añejo. When the drinks arrived five minutes later, she pushed one glass towards Bernice, and told her: "Drink up, in one swig." Bernice swallowed the drink and made a face as if she'd taken foul tasting medicine, while Kate slowly sipped her drink, obviously savouring it.

"We just had to run into those two, what a pity. How do you feel? A bit better? You looked as if you were going to drop right there on the sidewalk."

"I thought I was going to have a heart attack, or faint. Thanks for grabbing me; you're a lifesaver." She then began to cry softly, tears rolling down her cheeks. Kate looked for a tissue in her purse. "Oh, Kate, it was so awful seeing them. I'd never imagined them together, didn't want to think about it. If I pushed it away and didn't think about it, it might not be true. Do you think Tom is going to want a divorce?"

"I don't know what to say. I hope you don't fault me for saying it, but they looked really into each other. The best I can say is that you'll have to have patience. Tom is a good guy and he loves his children; you know that. Is he taking the kids to their games and practices like he said he would?"

"Yes, he does, and he's more punctual than before he left us." She stopped crying, wiping under her eyes for any traces with the tissue.

"Good. She really looks very young – really a kid. How much can they have in common? You surely don't think Tom would go clubbing with her? He'll get bored with her after the first gloss is gone from her pretty lips. It's probably a midlife crisis. He'll get over it. You're so good to him; he'll come back. You'll have to trust him, the person you fell in love with, although that might be too much to ask right now. If you want him to come back, you can't do anything hasty, Bernice. Come, lets go home."

———————

At the end of the evening, with the kids in bed and the movie already forgotten, Bernice checked her email. Anna had sent her a phone number and address for Gabriel Kalasnikoff – the last name he gave his two children. She picked up the phone in an impulse and punched the numbers. After two rings, somebody answered, and she almost put the phone down. "Hello?"

She took a deep breath, not knowing what would come out of her mouth. "Hi, yes, sorry I realize it's late. Would you like me to call back tomorrow? I'm Bernice Harrison. My husband and I adopted Shayla and Abby seven years ago."

"Oh." Silence on the other end.

Bernice's finger hovered over the end call button, when she heard the voice again and she put the phone back to her ear. "Yes?"

"Hi, sorry, I needed to think for a minute what to say. It's not that I don't remember who you are. I just don't know what to say. I feel terrible about what all has happened. From Anna I heard that the girls are doing alright."

"Please, don't apologize. I should, for calling this late. Yes, the kids are okay. It's just that your coming back into their lives, well, it's a bit sudden, and is actually complicating our lives. I would like to know what you had in mind. Anna emailed out of the blue; it was quite a shock." She waited.

"I'm sorry, I didn't mean to cause trouble. It's just that I want the girls to know that I love them and always have, but that I couldn't be anything but a problem to them, back then, being addicted and all, and wasn't in a good place. But that's all over now and I've been clean for coming up five years. I've got a job and I'm trying to help Nora's other kids, because I feel I have something to make up for. If at all possible, I wouldn't mind seeing the girls some time, if you would feel that would be all right."

Silence. For once in her life Bernice didn't know what to say. *Where is Tom when I need him?* A sigh escaped her, then she slowly started searching for words: "Well, uh, I'm not sure if this is a good time. You see, we have a few problems of our own right now. Uh, um, I'm in the middle of trying to make arrangements with my husband. Ah, well, he's at the moment not living at home; we have a bit of trouble, like I said."

"Oh, I'm so sorry. Is there anything I can do to help? I don't mean to cause trouble."

"That's all right, it's not your worry. We'll get through it. I know that Shayla really wants to be able to write to you or talk on the phone. I'm afraid she will have a lot of questions for you. I have protected the girls from too much information about Nora, and about you too, from what I knew then. Really, I don't know that much about you, and not at all about who you'd be now. Maybe we can start off really slow."

"Of course, I understand. I will tell you what you want to know about me; I have no secrets."

"I was going to tell Shayla more anyway, but she got angry with me. You know, she's a teenager. But she's been good all those years; I have to give her that, she has been a really good girl. Can I ask you to be careful what you tell her? She is quite down on herself sometimes and doesn't need to hear negative things about herself or about her family."

The voice responding sounded polite and a bit excited. "Of course not; I wouldn't tell her much, as that's all over and Nora is gone, so no need to say too much about that either."

"Thank you, Gabriel. Just one more thing, I also don't want you to lie or make things rosier, even when the truth is sometimes hard to take."

"You don't have to be afraid, Missus Harrison; I had a lot of counseling. In the treatment centre they showed us how to use our experiences and feelings as examples; we explored what we put our children though, when we weren't looking after them properly. Believe me, I'm still really hurting, thinking about what the girls were with Nora, and when I couldn't do anything about it. That's no excuse, but that's how it was. I wouldn't be surprised if the girls didn't want to know me at all."

Bernice felt her resistance weakening; he sounded reasonable, nice even. "Please, call me Bernice. Shayla is eager to meet you. I'd like to see you first and have some time to talk about my concerns and to get acquainted with you, before I can let you see the girls. You see, I love them, too; they're now part of our family. I don't want to see them hurt again."

"No, of course not. I don't want to see them hurt either. What did you have in mind?" "How about this. After we have met and after I had a chance to talk to my husband about it, I'll let her call you this week some time. What do you say, Gabriel?" She felt as if a heavy weight fell off her shoulders. It was not only up to her anymore.

"That's great, I'd really like that. Please, let me know when you want me to drop by. I have some vacation time coming. I can't think of anything better than to use my days off for this, but I would need a few days or so to give my boss notice."

Bernice arranged to meet Gabriel on Saturday morning at a Tim Horton's coffee shop.

She recognized him from his photos on Facebook Shayla had shown her: a handsome man – in a different way than Tom was. To her surprise, she had liked Gabriel after his first few sentences. She saw a clean cut man of slim stature in faded jeans, a light blue dress shirt and a navy blue jacket that were all new; his hair a short cut was graying at the temples while the rest of it was still shiny black. He seemed genuinely remorseful for his former life as an addict, expressed loathing for his inability to stand up to Nora and take charge, and for abandoning his young daughters when they needed him most. He eagerly listened to her own loving descriptions of his daughters. On leaving, she told him with a smile he'd passed the test.

After their meeting, Bernice could no longer hold on to her reasons to keep Gabriel from getting to know his daughters and she knew she'd have to invite him into her family's life, on a limited basis at first. He seemed like a quiet character, although responsive, with his alert eyes focused on her, trying to read her face while making an effort to answer Bernice's questions and concerns as thoroughly as he could.

She tried to anticipate what Abby and Shayla's responses would be to their biological father's return – the man who had put them into this world without any thoughts for their future. No doubt that Abby and Shayla would forgive him. More importantly, would *she* ever forgive him completely, and give him a fair chance? Time will tell. Bernice, as determined as ever, decided to tell the girls about Gabriel as soon as she would get home.

.

CHAPTER 22

Shayla's cell phone beeped – a text from Eric, great! She felt a rush washing over her and her heart was pumping hard in her chest. Then she read it: "I can't see you anymore, sorry. I guess we're not meant to be together." She read Eric's text message again and again, her heart rate slowing down, almost to a stop; all blood drained from her brain. Had she been standing, she would have fainted. She fell backwards on her bed, arms spread out sideways while breathing hard, whispering, "No, no, no, no…." Almost automatically she turned on her side and pulled her knees up to her chin into a fetal position, folding her arms tightly around her knees. She shivered, then broke out in a sweat and her tears started flowing silently.

Twenty minutes passed before she stopped crying and all thoughts had left her mind. Slowly, she got up and went to her vanity drawer in the bathroom and took her disposable shaver from it. She sat down on the bathroom floor and started cutting her underarm on the fleshy part between her wrist and elbow, pushing the shaver into her arm sideways, beside the older lacerations. A bit of blood was trickling down her arm; she looked at it, and cut another thin red line. Two thin stripes ran along the length of her arm.

Now the other arm. She had more difficulty getting the proper angle with her left, non-dominant hand and the cut was less effective. She pried off the protective plastic backing with a metal nail file, freeing the blade. Now the blood started dripping on the floor. A pretty, bright red circle was deepening in the middle of the virginally white bathmat underneath her. She felt her head floating, as if it had separated from her shoulders. She finally started to feel a dull pain radiating from the cuts. It felt good.

She reached for a towel, but it hung out of reach, so she got up. That was a mistake. She got dizzy and lost her balance, fell against the bathtub and hit her head on the rim with a dull thud. She faded out and crumbled to the floor, both her arms seeping drops of blood, slowly, drip by drip, forming two red flowers on the white mat. She noticed the blackness behind her closed eyes and then – nothing.

CHAPTER 23

When Bernice arrived home, she put her resolve into action before thinking it over too much and getting cold feet. She called out: "Shayla, Abby, where are you? I want to talk to you."

Abby called back: "Here, family room. I think Shayla's in her room."

"I want you to come to the living room, please." She went upstairs to Shayla's room, formulating sentences in her head, trying to find the best words to tell her daughters the news. Okay, Shayla wasn't in her room. She called again. "Shayla, where are you?"

She heard a movement in the bathroom and headed there, knocked on the door and entered right away. The scene she saw wasn't what she expected and she had trouble letting the vision enter her brain, but only for a few seconds, then she screamed: "Shayla, what have you done!" She knelt down on the floor beside Shayla, grabbed a towel from the towel bar, and wrapped it tightly around the arm that bled most.

Shayla lifted her head, just emerging from her fainting spell. "What?" When she saw the blood on the floor, smudged on the tiles, as well as the big stains on the mat, and she started crying. "I didn't mean to, I am so sorry, mom, I just, I just…."

"It's all right, sweetheart, I'm here. Don't worry, you'll be okay." She grabbed another towel and wrapped it around Shayla's other arm, then shouted: "Abby, bring the phone."

Understanding the urgency in her mother's voice Abby appeared 15 seconds later. "What's happened?" Bernice was holding her in a tight embrace. She was back to being practical.

"Abby, dial 911 and give me the phone and then stay downstairs to open the door when the ambulance arrived. Shayla cut herself." Bernice explained the situation and the 9-1-1 clerk told her the ambulance was on its way. In her quick scan of Shayla's arms before wrapping the towels, Bernice noticed the cuts were superficial and no arteries were hit, although quite a bit of blood had dripped onto the floor and the bath mat, making the actual damage look much worse than it was.

She helped Shayla get up from the floor, supporting her with an arm around her back, and softly spoke to her: "I understand you're in pain, honey. It'll get better, trust me. Did you take any drugs? The doctor would need to know. You can tell me."

"No, mom, I didn't. I just was so sad. I got a text from Eric; he dumped me. My friends hate me. My life sucks. I have nobody." She started crying again, which turned into wailing and then hyperventilating. Bernice stayed calm, and spoke softly to her daughter.

"Yes, honey, that's awful. You need to keep on breathing, sweetheart. Take a deep breath, in through your nose and out through your mouth. It will help you calm down, like this." She made Shayla breathe deeply and slowly, and Shayla calmed down somewhat, at least enough to stop wailing and finding her breath.

"I'm glad you didn't take any drugs. The cuts might have to get stitched up a bit, but I'll be with you." When the ambulance drove up, they both walked in and sat in the back, buckled in, as directed by the first responders.

The doctor confirmed that the cuts were superficial and needed very few stitches, but she wanted to make sure Shayla would see a psychiatrist as well, to assess risk for future self-harm, she said. The bump on her head was superficial, but just in case, she would need to have an x ray taken, so they waited for the nurse to write up the X ray acquisition in the cubicle.

It was an interesting wait. The white curtains between the cubicles were only partly drawn and she saw Shayla intently watch the scene in the cubicle next to Shayla's. They couldn't help but notice the pre-teen with a phobia for needles refuse the needle causing quite a ruckus, and heard all of the conversation between the girl – a foster child on the run with an abscessed tooth that needed to be treated – and the emergency nurse. The girl whimpered loudly, then hollered and swore at the nurse, who tried to put an intravenous needle in her arm as the young patient was trying to kick her away. At some point, the girl pulled her intravenous contraption completely out of her arm and announced she was leaving, although she apparently was already sedated, as in the next moment, she fell back onto the treatment table and passed out.

"You saw that, Mom?"

"Yes, honey; I wonder where her social worker was."

"I'm so lucky that I have you, Mom." Bernice smiled at her.

During the wait between seeing the triage nurse, the emergency doctor, and then the psychiatrist, Bernice and Shayla talked softly.

Shayla was tired felt and kept apologizing for her cutting, and for the drama of the ambulance. "In a way, I'm glad for what happened," she said.

"How so, Shayla?"

"I now know that I have a mom who loves me and will stand by me, whatever stupid things I might do, and that you are not angry with me. I feel so relieved, now the cat is out of the bag. I am failing and I won't graduate this year. I won't have no more secrets from you, Mom, I promise."

She sighed and hoped this was the last of the revelations. "Shayla, honey. We can talk later about school. I came home to tell you some good news about Gabriel. Do you want to hear it now?"

"Omigod, of course I do! What is it?" She perked up more and eagerly studied her mom's face.

"We met. Gabriel told me he's been five years clean from all drugs, is now in a good situation, and he has a job; from there on, we set up a visit for you girls with him at the house. What do you think, are you up to it, next week or so?"

Shayla's face shone. "Of course I'm up to it. Right. Like, that's all I ever wanted!" She snuggled up to Bernice, tears in her eyes. "At least I'll have my very own dad now and can see for myself, if he's like me. I hope I'm like him. He looks handsome on Anna's pictures"

"Yes, I think you might. We'll tell Abby when we get home."

———

They had been lucky that the emergency ward had been quiet that afternoon and within three hours they arrived back home. Bernice called Abby who joined them in the living room; she told Abby about her meeting with Gabriel and the plan for his visit meeting to get acquainted. Both her daughters had many questions that she tried to answer, as best she could. "Do I have to meet him?" Abby asked.

"No, sweetheart, only if you want to. It's really not something for doing in a hurry. We'll do that only when you're ready." Hearing Abby's response, she concluded that Abby had securely bonded with her and Tom, and a warm feeling grew inside her. In spite of it, she encouraged her anyway. "I just can't imagine you not being a tiny bit curious."

Abby shrugged. "I already have a dad; what do I need another dad for that I don't even know?" She looked defiantly at her sister, then at her mom. Bernice smiled at her.

"That's alright, honey."

"I just know we'll have lots to talk about." Shayla added, trying to be the big sister: "You'll see; you'll like him too. I just know it. You were so little and liked Bernice and Tom right away." Bernice watched her and noticed Shayla seemed to remember something. "I want to email Anna to tell her the good news. I can't wait. I'm so excited about meeting Gabriel after seven years. I do remember him, but not very well."

"Go ahead, honey, tell her. Anna will be happy too."

Later that day, when Tom dropped off the boys after their soccer games, he stepped inside for a few minutes to talk to her. Shayla heard their arrival and ran up to the kitchen to tell him the good news about Gabriel, but Tom's mind was still on hospital emergency that she'd called him about from the emergency department. He hugged Shayla and asked, "Are you okay, Shayla? I heard what happened and you being stitched up at the emergency. I am worried about you." He studied Shayla's face.

"I'm fine, Dad, don't worry. I was just having a sad day, right, because Eric dumped me. I felt, like, nobody loves me." She looked down at her hands, fidgeting at her nails.

"But, sweetheart, did you forget we love you?" Bernice noticed that Tom's voice had a tone of genuine surprise, while holding Shayla's shoulders and studying her face.

"It's like, you weren't around much, Dad, and I really didn't know why not, and besides, Mom can't do everything."

"Oh, well, you're right, sorry about not being here, sweetheart."

"And after my friends all dumped me, I felt, like, all alone. Mom was great and helped me. I promise I'll never cut myself again. It's so embarrassing. I learned my lesson, honestly."

After Shayla's confession, Tom let her shoulders go, put an arm around her, pulling her towards him and kissed the top of her head, then let her go. "I sure hope so. Okay then, I'll keep you to your promise."

"I'm so excited to meet Gabriel. Like, he's fine now, you know, and has a job and everything." Her eyes had a bright gleam and she enthusiastically turned towards Tom for a response.

"Your birth dad is fine, too? That is great news; the more people that love you the better, right? I'll try to be around more often. How about I take everybody out for dinner tomorrow?"

Bernice heard in his voice that he was trying to be supportive to Shayla. He walked towards the kitchen, making sure she was paying attention to his conversation with Shayla. He looked at her with a question in his eyes. She kept her face expressionless as she was thinking that they didn't need his charity, but instead of a snappy answer, she replied coolly: "That sounds fine. Where will you take us?"

"Wherever you all want to go."

Abby shouted excitedly, "I want to go to the new Mario place. To Mario's."

The boys chimed in. "Yes, pizza!"

"Me too."

"Okay, Mario's it is. You okay with it, Bernice?"

"Sure." She didn't look him in the eye and pretended to be busy, rummaging in the cabinets for a pot. When she looked up, she heard Shayla ask for his support beyond words.

"Dad, would you please come to court with me on Wednesday? I'm scared. I want you there, please, if you don't mind?"

She observed the happy reunion of Shayla and Tom with unease, wondering if he would follow through on his promises this time. Tom put an arm around Shayla and looked genuinely chastised when he replied. "Of course I'll go with you, sweetheart. I'm honoured that you want me there. You've had a rough time of it this last while, and I want to be there for you. I'm sorry that I haven't been there as much as I could've."

"No problem, Dad. I'm happy you're not mad at me."

She saw Shayla pulling her dad's arm through hers and kissing him on his cheek; although she didn't trust Tom, Shayla's obvious happiness reverberated in her too. Tom looked at her, eyebrows raised and a question in his eyes, but he didn't ask her anything. She just nodded her head twice, her eyes meeting his, as Tom and Shayla walked together to the back door. "Well, it's time for me to go. See you all tomorrow at five; be there or be square."

"Oh Dad, *you* are square," Shayla laughed, and happily darted down the stairs to her room. Daniel and Jon said their goodbyes and went to the family room to play their video game. Abby said she'd set up the Barbie House in her own room, as she was tired of the boys' fights, she said. The children all out of earshot, Bernice finally spoke up from the kitchen. "That was great how you approached Shayla; she needed that. Thank you, Tom. See you tomorrow." She smiled again and turned around to fill the pot with water.

"My pleasure. I hope we can talk about all of this some day soon. I don't know anymore what's going on in my family and I would like to know."

Avoiding his stare, Bernice dove with her head into the fridge looking for vegetables, as she gave him the boot out the door. "I don't have to remind you that was your choice, Tom. Bye then, see you tomorrow." He turned back to look back at her and smiled, but she didn't see it. Wordless, Tom left the house through the backdoor.

CHAPTER 24

O n Wednesday, Shayla found out that the court hearing wasn't quite as intimidating as it had sounded. They waited around in the lobby of the courthouse until her name was called. Her dad pushed her ahead of him towards an office off to the side of the main entrance. A rather plain-looking woman introduced herself as the trial coordinator, and the court clerk sitting next to her gave her a court date for the first appearance in a month.

Another hour was left of class time. Instead of dropping her off to school, her dad took her for a treat to the Dairy Queen, where they talked more about her expectations for her upcoming meeting with Gabriel. At one point she asked him something she had often thought about, but never dared to ask him before, and bluntly asked him: "Why did you decide to adopt us, Dad?" She studied his face, making sure he wouldn't just send her on a side-track; she'd had enough of his patronizing dad-attitude. She wanted the facts.

"Well, uh, your mom wanted to adopt you both and I wanted what she wanted, because I loved her – and still do – so I agreed. Our boys were two and four and we both always wanted more than two kids, so you and Abby made our family complete. Besides, you were cute girls and really needed a home. Why do you ask?" She decided his answer seemed genuine, although corny.

"Well, Dad, if it's true what you say, I wondered, like, why you changed your mind, or did you, like, even think about us, when you decided to leave Mom; you left us too. You get my question, right?" She couldn't stop her hands from fussing with her face and her hair, startled by her own boldness. All of a sudden, she wasn't sure whether she even wanted to hear the answer.

He looked away from her, hesitating with his answer. "Ouch, that hurts, but it's a fair question. I don't know what to say." He stayed quiet.

Shayla jumped into the silence. "Dad, you really hurt me when you left; like, you are the second dad who did that. I thought you didn't not love us anymore. I also thought it was my fault, that things were too difficult with two extra kids, but Mom said it has nothing to do with Abby or me. I know, it's not all about me, but still…." She couldn't look at him now, afraid for the answer; Tom just stared at her, wide-eyes, trying to come up with an answer.

Again she spoke, hurriedly, as if she would scare herself, if she slowed down and fail to finish her sentence. "Of course, Mom was very hurt, too," Shayla continued. "She's been moping around ever since and I've heard her cry in her room very often, almost every night since you left. What happened between you two, anyway?"

She was entitled to an answer, she figured, but was also afraid she made him angry with her line of questioning. She studied his face. What she saw surprised her. Her dad seemed to be deep in thought and not upset. Something akin to shyness came over him; he looked positively embarrassed.

"Mmm, uhh, I can't tell you, sweetheart; that's between me and mom. Maybe one day you'll understand that people grow apart some-times. It's not about loving you and Abby and the boys less, not at all. I love you all just as much as before, maybe even more now than before; I miss you all so much. I realize now that I took you all for granted and was selfish. I found out how much I hate being apart from you all. I miss our breakfasts together on the weekends, and going out for family dinners, and our vacations together, the walks in the mountains. Well, you know what I mean, don't you?" He searched his daughter's face, eager for her understanding.

"Yes, totally. I know exactly what you mean; I miss that, too, Dad. You're really the first dad I had who did those things with us as a family. It was wonderful. I want a family like that of my own when I'm ready. I'm glad you said that, Dad, about loving us."

Shayla's eyes shone brightly as she pulled her chair closer to Tom's. She dug into her DQ Mint Oreo Blizzard with delight. Tom looked at her while drinking his coffee. "At last I did something right today," he said to her. She smiled back with her gorgeous grin.

On the day of Gabriel's visit, Shayla woke up with strong feelings of anticipation. Her mom looked rather uncomfortable, but she was elated, granted, with a bit of confusion around its edges, as she was not sure what she wanted from Gabriel. She had told her mom that it would depend on who he turned out to be and how they got along. When Gabriel rang the doorbell at exactly the agreed on time in the afternoon, she rushed upstairs from her bedroom catching up to her mom by the front door. At the last minute, she stepped back behind her mother.

Gabriel was all dressed up in what appeared to be brand new clothes, a fold still in his cotton-twill pants. He was looking good, she thought. Her mom opened the door wide, welcoming him with "Hi Gabriel, come in," and he stepped inside the house, while Mom slowly closed the door behind him, immediately turned around, and pulled her forward by an arm, laying an arm around her shoulders. "This is our beautiful daughter, Shayla, all grown up since you last saw her."

Standing beside Bernice, unsure what to do, she felt herself frozen on the spot. Next, in slow motion, she lifted her arm and reached out her hand to Gabriel, as the correct gesture. Luckily, her mom took the initiative speaking up, as Gabriel apparently was much like her – at a loss of what to do in a situation like this. "Shayla, honey, I think it would be okay, if you wanted to hug Gabriel. Isn't it, Gabriel? But, only if you want to." Gabriel nodded.

She suddenly felt her muscles melting, and she threw her arms around the man who looked so much like her, with the same dark hair, the same amber-coloured eyes, and a similar, tall body. She felt Gabriel gently putting his arms around her, keeping some distance between them. He was only an inch or so taller than her, she noticed. They stood there for a few moments, arms around each other. Time stood still. That feeling was unbelievable, so magical, as if the walls around her melted.

CHAPTER 25

When they let go of each other, she noticed her face was wet with tears. She looked through her tears at Gabriel, who quickly wiped the back of his hand across his cheeks. Omigod, he was crying too! Her mom didn't say anything and just handed her the box of tissues, and then started walking decisively down the hall towards the family room, and when she took the five treads, she looked over her shoulder at her, which she took as the sign to follow, and she started to walk up the stairs too.

When she looked in turn back over her shoulder, she saw that Gabriel was following them. They all sat down in the family room. Her mom started babbling, playing the hostess. "Well, it has been a while, hasn't it? They grow up so fast, don't they? Shayla was very eager to see you, Gabriel. I will tell you now that Shayla had a bit of a rough go this last week – didn't you, sweetheart – and she is a bit emotional right now. I'll get Abby to join us; you two can chat and get reacquainted." She disappeared.

Embarrassed, she started talking. "Don't mind her; she's nervous, and don't worry about me crying; I cry easily, but I'm OK." She smiled; it helped and she stopped crying.

"I'm so happy that I get to see you, Shayla," Gabriel finally said with a tremble in his deep voice. "You can call me Gabriel; I don't expect you to call me Dad. I haven't been a dad. I don't want to intrude on your family and I completely respect your bond with Bernice and Tom. I'm very grateful for the home and the love they've given you and Abby. I couldn't have done that for you and your sister."

She grabbed a tissue and wiped her face dry, without much effect, as his words seemed to trigger her tears that wouldn't stop flowing, even when she smiled. She managed to squeeze a few words out, "I'm so happy, too. I don't know why I can't stop crying."

"That's okay; I feel emotional, too. There were times I didn't think I was going to make it through treatment, afraid I'd never see you and Abby again. I'm very grateful you want to see me. Thank you for seeing me." Gabriel's head was down and he looked like a heap of misery.

Shayla's head jerked up and her eyes dried instantly, for the moment. "Why wouldn't I want to see you? Of course I want to see my dad."

"You must be angry at me for not showing up earlier in your life. Now you're all grown up and I wasn't there for you all this time. I won't blame you for being angry; you have a right to resent me."

Just then, Bernice and Abby entered, and the introduction procedure repeated itself. Abby's response to meeting him was completely different from hers. While keeping her distance, but like a well-trained girl Abby politely said: "Hi, nice to meet you."

Hearing this, she couldn't help herself and snorted, which caused her mom to frown and throw her a warning glance. Abby paused several meters away from Gabriel and waited. Gabriel took a few steps forward bridging the gap, and then carefully embraced her for a second, quickly and lightly, and then stepped back. Abby stiffly endured the hug, not hugging back, an expression of surprise on her face. Bernice started the conversation, as the good moderator she was.

"Okay, what would you all like to do? How about if we get the conversation going first and you tell us a bit of what happened in your life? Then you could talk to the girls in private later, if you like."

"Sounds like a good idea. Where to start? What would you like to know?" He glanced at shyly at her. Abby sat on the couch beside her mom, an arm through hers, holding on tightly.

Her mom – always practical – suggested: "The girls last saw you at Wanda's home a few days after Nora's funeral. What happened afterwards? We knew you were living before that at a farm and had come back to town for court, stayed in a shelter, and that you and Nora had split up years before."

"Sure. After I saw you both first at the funeral, I felt really bad for leaving you two behind with strangers. In all fairness, I couldn't have looked after you, as a drug addict. All I could do was look forward to my next fix. I was a mess. But, I never forgot my daughters and there weren't enough drugs to ban you two from my mind. After our last visit at your foster home, I decided I would get clean. It took me several years to get clean and stay that way. But, now I think I've got it; I have something to do – a great job – and I hardly ever have cravings anymore and never any that I don't know how to handle."

"Oh, Gabriel, that is great. Good for you." Her mom couldn't help herself.

"After volunteering in the outreach program for a long time, I was hired as a counsellor. I'm going to night classes to get my diploma. I found myself a good apartment and I am stable and healthy. This has been going on for the last half year, so I thought maybe I could get my girls back into my life in some way, maybe just visiting. Of course, only if you both want to see me. I'd totally get it, if you said no. I'm so sorry for everything that happened to you."

She hung on to her birth dad's every word, soaking up the information that reverberated deep inside her, words she didn't know she had craved for years. While talking, his face was wet with tears, just like her own; she hadn't even realized her face was wet and dripping, until she noticed his.

Her mom put the box of tissues next to him and said: "That's okay, Gabriel; it's emotional for all of us. What is your connection to Nora's world? Could you tell us?" She looked encouraging, with a smile on her face. Gabriel looked down at his hands. Although his voice was trembling, he continued talking, spilling the sad story, of how he realized he never really was in a relationship with Nora; she was using him, and wouldn't let him see the girls. He then broke off all contact with her and left to live with his family on the farm.

When he came back to town years later, he didn't think Bill was a suitable caregiver, but he didn't know what to do about it. With a sincere voice, his hands still trembling, but with dry eyes he said: "Bernice, I was really happy when you got involved. That meant that at least somebody decent would look after my girls and that Nora had no say anymore." Hearing this, she couldn't help herself and cried fullout, without sound. She clasped her hands tightly, white-knuckled, to stop herself, but anger fuelled her, anger at this woman she loved that was only thinking about herself, anger at herself to not having seen this earlier.

Her mom had listened intently to what Gabriel had to say, but was looking at her now. "Are you alright Shayla?"

"Don't mind me, I can't help it, Mom." Her mom grabbed her hand and held on to it. Then Abby piped up. "Why was our uncle that looked after us, not a good man? What was wrong? I liked him and he was good to us and they took us away from him and from my mom. That was not right."

Her mom spoke slowly, but minced no words, for which she was grateful, as she didn't have the guts to tell Abby herself.

"Sweetheart, the man didn't shop for food and let Shayla buy fast food only, but Shayla was too young to be your mother. Uncle's home was filthy, unsanitary, unsafe for children and Nora paid a caretaker to look after you. Tim had all kinds of medical problems and one of them was a bad heart, plus he was drinking every day, and drunk by nightfall. It's a miracle that no worse had happened to either one of you. You both hardly went to school and were way behind in your classes. Let's leave it at that, okay? Sorry I had to be this blunt, sweetheart, but you might as well know too."

Abby gasped as her mom was talking and then spoke up, as she let go of her mom's arm and looked at her incredulously. "Nobody ever told me that. I was mad that I had to do all kinds of things at your house, like cleaning up my room, and that Uncle was gone. Why didn't you tell me about everything?"

"Well, baby, you were just little, six years old, for goodness sakes. You just needed a cuddle and somebody to love you. That, we did, I hope."

After Abby had her say, she needed to say her piece and spoke up, and her voice came out clear and strong. "Mom, I remember. I was so lonely. I felt sorry for Abby, and I had to be her mom too. It was so awful, Uncle getting sick every night and falling on the floor. Once, I called 911 and he got mad at me the next day and wouldn't speak to me for a week. I missed my mom and wanted to see her, but she never came." She started weeping again.

She felt her mom sit down on the couch's arm rest and put an arm around her: "Go on, let it all out, sweetheart, it's okay."

"I thought she didn't love us; why else did didn't she visit us more often? I thought it was my all my fault that my mom had better things to do. Then she died without saying goodbye. I really loved her and she looked so different in that casket."

Gabriel got up from his seat and sat down next to her on the other side, grabbed her hand and held it between both his hands. Bernice had drawn Abby close to her, an arm protectively around Abby's small body; they were all sitting pressed together on the couch. Somehow that felt right. Taking deep breaths to keep on talking, she had released the things she had always pushed away, the thoughts that made her feel bad and had kept hidden for all those years.

"Like, I was scared all the time. Then when Abby and I came to your house, all I wanted was for you to like me and I wanted to be good. Like, I was good, but I was always afraid, like, you and Dad would send me away some day. I thought it was my fault that Dad left us. It's too hard to look after all of us, to have to think about all those things. I'm so tired, Mom. Can you forgive me? I've done so many bad things, but I just wanted you to love me."

Her mom grabbed both her arms and pulled her up from the couch and said with a stern voice: "Shayla, that's now all over. We start with a clean slate. Stand up, let me give you a hug. No more tears now. It's all over."

They hugged. She felt her mom's arms tightly around her, and she talked softly in her ear, repeating over and over, "It's okay, it's okay,

don't worry, it's okay," until she had calmed down; she had no tears
left to cry.

They all sat in silence for a while, thrown off by all the emotion,
spilled over after years of managing to control any leakage of those
deep fears. Gabriel sat with eyes wide, staring at Bernice. Then he softly
started speaking.

"I had no idea, I'm so sorry, Shayla, that you had to go through
this. And you, too, Abby, as I am sure you loved Tim. I promise, from
now on I will be there for you two and you can tell me anything and
everything, and I will never judge you, ever. From now on, I will do my
best to make things better for you."

Bernice softly replied. "Thank you, Gabriel. I had no idea either."
Then she turned to Shayla. "I always suspected you kept a lot inside,
sweetheart. I'm glad it came all out. I would never, ever send you away.
When we adopted you girls, Tom and I made a commitment *for life*.
We chose you because we really wanted you both in our family, and we
do love you both very much."

She felt embarrassed. "It's quite silly, isn't it? I feel so immature."

"Don't feel bad: This is another hurdle most adopted children will
face – always thinking it was their fault. But, we know that's not true,
and that Nora and Gabriel simply could not look after you, for reasons
that have nothing to do with you. I'm going upstairs to make us something to drink and eat. You can stay here girls, I would like some time
alone with Gabriel, if that's alright."

She saw that Gabriel looked at her mom with a sense of grati-
tude, even admiration, and he nodded his head vigorously. "Thank
you, Bernice."

Standing by the top of the stairs, her mom had to say something else. "There's just one more thing I want to point out, if it's not clear already: That Dad left, well, he and I are having some problems, like most couples do at some point in their marriage. I hope we can work it out. I know he misses all of you, children very much."

She had one more thing to clear up as well. "But, what I've done was bad, stealing, lying and doing drugs. When I got caught, I was very afraid that I screwed up with you."

"Of course not, but that doesn't mean that your mistakes don't have consequences; they do. But you're allowed to make a few mistakes. How else are you supposed to learn? Your job is to learn from your mistakes. We, parents, will just have to teach you other ways of dealing with stresses and fears. That's our job. So, that's why I'm glad it all came out. Now we all know what you're dealing with. Good for you; being honest is the beginning of all good relationships. Gabriel is lucky to get to see the real you, right from the start."

She saw Gabriel exchange a look with her mom that she didn't understand. He nodded, then looked at her: "I'm honoured that you would show yourself to me, Shayla. Thank you. Can I give you a hug?" She got up and dry-eyed now, she smiled and softly said "yes", walked towards Gabriel, and finally at peace, she hugged him.

CHAPTER 26

Having cooked breakfast for the both of them, Tom read the newspaper on his tablet, when Marla asked a question out of the blue: "What are we planning for Christmas?" He looked up from his tablet and glanced into her direction and without making any effort to formulate a reply, shrugged his shoulders, making sure he kept his face blank.

She threw her fork on the table that hit the plate with a sharp clatter. "How come you never go there?"

He startled upright, but still kept looking at his screen. "What do you mean, go where?"

"You know damn well what I mean. Look at me. I asked you what your plans are for the Christmas holidays and you're avoiding an answer."

He glanced quickly at her. "Oh, that," and kept quiet, while pretending to read his iPad.

"Well, what's your answer?" Marla pressed on. "It's only a month away and we'll have to start shopping, and I want to ask my mom to join us for dinner. She's lonely after Dad died; I want to ask her to stay for a week, or so. What do you think?" Her demanding voice had an edge; he suspected it could turn into whining, or even crying any minute now.

He couldn't escape answering any longer and took a deep breath, exhaled, looking at Marla's chin: "Well, what can I say? It depends on Bernice and what she's planning. Now that my daughters' birth father is in the picture, I'm not sure what will happen. I haven't got a definite role anymore and just am a fill-in dad."

He threw his tablet on the table and felt like getting up, but willed himself to stay in his seat. His view of Marla had changed from when they first had met, although he guessed she probably didn't know why. He had to be assertive with her and needed some more distance, was less willing to bend to whatever she wanted.

Marla pushed on without mercy. "Then you should find out. Soon. I'm planning an early Christmas dinner, say around four in the afternoon, and on Christmas Eve my mother will want to go to church. You should come with us; she would like that. We need to buy presents for everybody. Would you like some help with buying gifts for your kids? I plan on having our gift opening after Christmas dinner. They can come for dinner, if they like."

"Can we drop it, please? I'll give you an answer tonight. I promise." He wasn't into all of that and Bernice usually took care of those arrangements anyway, and so much more competently than Marla. He quickly finished his breakfast and walked away from her, with a mumbled excuse of preparing to go to work. He couldn't help thinking he should look into a transfer for Marla to another office.

As a self-confessed tightwad – he preferred to call himself parsimonious – Tom minded his small change, especially since he now had to cough up a big child maintenance cheque each month since the separation. He had insisted to share all household costs fifty-fifty when he moved in with Marla –didn't want to be called a loafer – and suggested to give Marla rides – didn't need to take two vehicles to work – but now regretted the arrangement.

The fuss about Christmas made him cranky. He missed home; he missed Bernice, and most of all the kids, *especially* with Christmas. Bernice told him she had asked Gabriel to join the family for Christmas. That man had no business playing father to his kids. She also had told him that when Gabriel first came to the house to meet the girls, Shayla had something of an emotional breakthrough. He had missed it; he missed all of the important things in his family, lately.

He had met Gabriel a few weeks earlier at the house – his house – when dropping off the boys at Bernice's on a Saturday after their games, and he had stayed for a few minutes longer. His boys greeted Gabriel enthusiastically, calling him Uncle Gabriel, and they left Tom behind at the door without saying their goodbyes, eager to take the man down to the family room. He had to call them back and asked for a hug.

If Gabriel would have looked at him wrong, or had said a wrong word, he would've punched him in the face, to pay him for all he failed to do when the girls needed a father. The man was a handsome devil, that much Tom conceded. Hell, he wouldn't be surprised, if Bernice had the hots for him. What if Gabriel moved into his territory? Or rather – what *used* to be his territory.

He couldn't get his family out of his head on the way to work. Things with Marla weren't going as well as he had envisioned it at the start of their adventure. She kept pressuring him for a commitment, he assumed she meant a wedding. He had no desire to go through all of that again, still married – to Bernice, but Marla wasn't letting up.

It was becoming clear to him that Marla was not somebody he would marry. She was too bossy, too shallow, wanted a family, which he did not; he already had one. Why would he get married again, anyway? Maybe it was time to reconsider what he was doing with his life. While Marla chattered, he started making an inventory of what he wanted, in preparation for his speech to Bernice, which he knew he was going to have, soon.

Life with Marla wasn't much fun anymore. In a cranky mood, he judged Marla's earlier passion for sex as a lure to get what she wanted, and generally, that would cost him money. When he was in a more generous mood, he ascribed her manipulation to her youth and insecurity; she hadn't yet developed her own sexual needs.

Maybe it was time to let her grow up and meet somebody her own age, time for him to be fair to her. He should instead focus on his kids and getting them through school. He quickly glanced sideways to look at Marla's face. She was silent now, mouth drawn down, a frown on her brow.

A week ago, Shayla had called him. "Hi Dad, I'm just calling to tell you don't have to come to court anymore with me. I have asked Gabriel to come. He wanted to be there for me." Unhappy about being put in second place, he nevertheless came up with an answer, realizing he was losing his spot in her life. "Alright honey, whatever you want. Are you sure? You're not just afraid to say no to him?"

"No of course not. He knows about court and such things; he can help me."

He was sure Gabriel's presence in court would be to her detriment; he would have made a better impression on the judge, had he stood by his daughter. After that call, he had been unreasonably angry for a minor error by one of his clerks on documents.

Just yesterday, he heard from Bernice that Shayla got sentenced to time in community service with six months' probation. Had he been there in court with her, he would've gotten her off after testifying to Shayla's character as an actual father. She needed a strong male in her life to keep her safe, especially since she was emotionally quite a mess this past year.

He narrowly missed a bicyclist while turning a right corner. Oops, better pay more attention to traffic. Uncharacteristically, Marla still sat quietly beside him. Recovering from the near-miss, his thoughts returned to his family.

Abby had asked him when he would be coming home to them, to be a family again. Abby, his sweet little darling. She was still a child, and so trusting. It was a miracle that after all she has been through she still was so innocent and affectionate to him. She hadn't taken to Gabriel with the same instant karma as Shayla. He smiled and started to feel better.

When his parents divorced, he wasn't even a teen and had missed his dad terribly the following. When Bernice became pregnant, he told her he wanted to be actually present in his kids' lives. Another failed promise. Even while making an effort to stay involved with his kids, he could no longer pretend he was an active and present father. Taking the boys twice a week to soccer wasn't enough to qualify. Especially Jon was missing him and had asked him many times before when he was coming home, but stopped asking.

They had arrived at the real estate building. He helped Marla out of the vehicle and holding her by her elbow steadying her on her high heels – as had become his habit – they entered the office together. Everything looked normal.

That night on the couch watching TV, Marla refused his affections that usually would lead to sex. She pushed him away and moved over to the other seat across the couch. "I'm not ready for sex, Tom. You haven't yet told me what we're doing with Christmas."

He didn't pursue her as usual. Looking straight into her eyes and with an unusual coolness in his voice he asked: "Look at me. You're using sex to get what you want from me. What happened to that sexy girl, who couldn't wait to get in bed with me – what am I saying – in the back of the car, on the beach, really anywhere, for hot and passionate sex? You were insatiable and made me feel like a young stud. Tell me, what happened, Marla?"

"I'm not dignifying that with an answer." She turned her eyes away from him, crossed her legs and starting moving her foot up and down in quick repetitions, eyes on the TV screen.

"But dear girl, you should answer; it's a valid concern. I don't think my sex drive has changed, but yours has. Why?"

"Well, if you must know, it's been a year and I don't just want to be your lover anymore. I want to get married and have kids, but you haven't asked me to be your wife. You even left your wife for me and should get a divorce. Why don't you go ahead with it? What's wrong? Don't you want me to be your wife? Am I not good enough?"

He watched her without answering. She stopped moving her foot and slumped somewhat in her seat, shoulders resting against the back rest of the armchair, and she started crying softly. She grabbed a tissue from the end table and dabbed the space under her eyes, trying not to disturb her mascara. Then she got up and walked to the bedroom, with a straight back and her head lifted in a majestic walk of contempt.

Tom braced himself, but decided to take this moment, thanking his lucky stars. He followed her into the bedroom and sat down beside her on the double bed, where she had flung herself into a tempting pose, on her stomach, turning her upper body towards him, leaning on her elbow. He took her free hand in both of his and looked at her tear-stained face, addressing the issue in a gentle voice.

"Well, honey, since you asked the question, I think you deserve an honest answer. I've been thinking lately about whether we would be a good match or not, and I have to conclude: We are not. I don't want any more children; I've got four already. You want kids, completely understandable, as you don't have any yet, and you are young. You want to be married. I can't honestly do that, as I feel I'm not completely finished with my marriage to Bernice, but I'm not sure what's going to happen next. To be really honest, I was thinking about – maybe – reconciling with her, for the kids' sake, if she wants me back. I don't expect you to understand that. Maybe later you will."

Marla's eyes opened wide, she got up, and ran into the bathroom, wailing loudly; she locked the door behind her. Shit, that didn't go so well, he concluded, while walking to the bathroom door; he knocked softly and in the gentlest voice he could muster, he asked, "Honey, please, let me hold you, I didn't want to hurt you, but we were talking, so I have to be honest with you; please, come out, please, please?"

After several minutes, the door opened a crack and Marla peered through the gap. "You are breaking up with me. What's left to talk about?" She opened the door wider and stepped into the bedroom. Tom took her into his arms and caressed her head, her soft, blonde locks. It felt to him like he was consoling his daughter.

"There, there," he said while Marla softly wept.

CHAPTER 27

Since Gabriel Kalasnikoff had come back into her life, Shayla had become close with Anna. They had become like real sisters, sharing gossip and details about people in their lives and about herself, face to face on Skype. When they compared their reactions to Gabriel's reappearance, Shayla found out these were similar to her own, and after confessing her particular flashbacks of the most dramatic episodes in her life with Nora, she found out that Anna also had experienced those for years afterwards. Both had even accepted their distorted ideas of what a parent was from Nora's example.

Overcome with regret, pain, and anger about losing a parent at an early age – feelings they had stuffed and denied for so many years – the girls shared their childhood stories of loneliness, of lacking somebody that held them and soothed them when they needed it most. Anna shared that she had started to realize that her ingrained tendency to self-blame came from this past – a characteristic Shayla immediately recognized.

That evening, Shayla was on the computer having a conversation face-to-face on Skype with Anna who played the elder sister to her, just like she used to do for Abby.

"Although I like Gabriel too, you should realize that he cannot possibly do what we want him to do – undo all of that past hurt. He's just one man, and besides, he had a life himself that wasn't the greatest. He's just back on his feet and building a life of his own."

"I know that; I'm just grateful he came into my life, especially now that my dad and my mom have troubles. They might get a divorce." Her eyes filled with tears and she swallowed vigorously to force them back.

"That's too bad. Sorry to hear that. You'd think I might come and visit you one day? I would like to give you a hug now." Her grainy picture on Shayla's screen showed a young woman intently staring into the camera at a point above Shayla's eyes.

"That would be great. I'll ask my mom. I'm feeling sort of confused; one day I'm up, the next day I'm down. I got my first broken heart, and still feel so low thinking about Eric. I'm too down on myself, my mom tells me. At least I have a counselor now and she helps me a lot. She said I am still processing the losses in my life."

"Does it help, seeing a counsellor?" asked Anna.

"Yes, it really helps. Really it does. I want to become just like you. You're strong and you have a girl yourself, right? I want to be a mother and I'll never leave my child, whatever happens."

Anna chuckled. "Don't kid yourself, Shayla. You're strong, too, and you'll get through this. You should talk to Bernice about all this; she seems very nice."

"Right, like, she's my rock; we do talk. She was great, like when Gabriel first came to our house. You know, I would like so much for my dad, I mean my adoptive dad, to come back to, like, live with us, just as before, as it's all a little much for my mom on her own. I thought it was, like, very bad of him to take off with that skank from his work.

Omigod, like, what a dink, but I do like him. Men – you can't trust them." Spoken with the certainty of an experienced teen.

"Hey Shayla, not all men are like that. Look at your dad, I mean Gabriel. He never wanted to leave you guys, but Nora shut him out. Nora was just bad news for any man. It's just that us girls need to pick the right man, right? Be more critical. Not fall in love so easily, like, be more proud. Hey, do you think that Gabriel likes your mom? Wouldn't that just be cool if they got together?"

Shayla ignored Anna's last remark. She had some news to tell Anna that was burning on her lips. "You know what? I met a guy, he's asking me out; his name is Shane. He's nice. Like, I don't know if I can trust him, so I've been giving him the brush-off. He's graduating with me next year. Shane seems nice; he's in hockey and is sort of a jock, but not really."

"What next year. I thought that was this year?"

"It's a drag, but graduating this year was too much with all that's been going on, like, I don't want to bust my chances for university with low grades, so I am taking another year. I would fail most of my courses."

"Oh, you're right, Shayla. But that's good news about Shane, you said? You should check him out first, see what he's like, then ask him to the grad next year. Is he on Facebook? I want to check. You'd feel better about leaving school, if you had somebody that also left at the same time. It sounds like you've got over that jerk Eric."

"Yeah, just about. He turned out to be the guy from The Paper Bag Princess – unworthy of the princess' love; I got that book from my mother when I was little. Do you know that book? My counsellor says I shouldn't hurry into any relationship right now, until I feel stronger and more secure in myself." She laughed with embarrassment.

"Oh, well, what do they know?" Anna snorted. "As long as you take it easy."

"Yeah, right. Got to go, my mom is calling for supper. Love you, see you soon."

From Gabriel, she learned about his heritage: Doukhobor from the south – she had to look up what that meant – spirit wrestler, the name signifying the struggle for a better life with help from the power of love, swearing off any form of violence or coercion. He was raised in farming country, in the middle of Doukhobor communities established by his migrant ancestors, refugees from Russia persecuted for their religion, because the Russian Orthodox Church considered them heretics.

When she read that on Wikipedia, she instantly loved that history – her history – and she identified immediately with the belief in gentleness and its old world history of persecution and diaspora. She learned that when Gabriel was living with his parents and his disabled brother, the villagers had already slowly dispersed and most of the farms had been sold. His parents and his brother had since died. Gabriel didn't know whether any other relatives were left elsewhere. Oh well, she now had two families and two dads, and that was enough for her.

CHAPTER 28

Bernice decided to cook a quick dinner of stir-fry veggies with left over chicken with pasta. She dumped a pack of whole wheat noodles in a pot with boiling water and then stirred the veggies, already braising in the wok. The prepared sauce was heating up in the microwave and it beeped. She gave it another five minutes. The boys liked noodles and they deserved a bit of attention, Bernice figured. She called out to Abby in the downstairs family room playing a solitary video game. "Honey, please tell the boys and Shayla to come to dinner." Abby ran off to do as she was told.

The phone rang. It was Tom.

"Hi. Did I get you at a bad time? I can call back." His voice sounded a bit tight. She tensed as well and a sense of looming disaster took over.

"No, that's okay, go ahead. I'm cooking dinner, but I can listen." Bernice turned down the gas flame under the pots and grabbed the wall calendar, ready to write down any new entries for their plans with the kids that Tom might come up with, then sat down at the breakfast bar. "What's up?" she asked.

"Bernice, I'd like to talk about a few things, but not over the phone. You got any time this week? And I want to talk about Christmas; Marla wants to do a mid-afternoon dinner with Christmas and the gift giving with the children after that. Would that work for you? She would like an answer tonight. Sorry to drop this on you now."

"No problem. I haven't really thought about the details yet, but, the afternoon is fine. We do Christmas gifts early in the morning anyway; if you remember, the kids can't hold off very long unwrapping their gifts. When do you propose to meet? I've got only Friday this week; I don't do any driving of kids then. Or, we could meet for lunch that day." The thought flashed through her mind it might have something to do with Gabriel. "How about we meet at the Train Station pub at 5 p.m.?"

"Yes, that works. Thanks, Bernie. I appreciate it. Marla and I will then have the kids in the afternoon at Christmas." Tom had called her Bernie, his nickname that only he was allowed to use, and that he hadn't used since he'd left her. Uh, what could that mean?

Bernice and Tom sat across from each other in the pub, she with a glass of Merlot in front of her, and he with a beer. He was thinner than he used to be and dressed more spiffily, Bernice observed. Tom was shifting in his seat every minute or so. Obviously, each was uncomfortable, but Bernice was the one to say it. "Yes, it's rather awkward," Tom agreed.

It had been a long time since they had been together like this, and at the same time, it was strangely familiar. They each looked around to see if anybody they knew was around to spot them. Only strangers were looking back. Finally, Tom said, "You might wonder what this is about?"

"I'm curious, I have to admit. But I have patience, I can wait."

"No need to wait. I might as well come right out with it. Since we spoke last on the phone, Marla and I broke up. I'll move out as soon as I find another space; I'm looking, shouldn't be too long. We both were already unhappy with how things were between us, and a break up had been coming for a while."

"Oh, Tom! What can I say? She must be heartbroken." Bernice shifted on the edge of her chair.

"Yes, she took it hard. I've been thinking about talking with you for a while. I would very much like for us to try again, patch things up between us. That's why I wanted to talk with you in person. Don't give me an answer right away; take your time. I wouldn't blame you if you'd tell me to take a hike. I deserve that. And I have to find a place to stay yet." He sat back into his chair, waiting for the rejection, his fists clenched inside his pockets.

Bernice's eyes focused on his face and she held her breath for a few seconds. "My God, that's a strange turn. What brought that on? I'd have to think about that; that option hadn't entered my mind when you called; that's for sure."

Tom quickly replied. "Does that mean you won't consider it?" He keenly studied her face, sitting now straight in his chair, no slumping.

"To be frank, at first I missed you tremendously. I missed having someone, an adult in my life; you know I've always liked being with you. But, later on, getting help from Gabriel with babysitting gave me more options for when I wanted to go out with my friends, or go to the gym, do things for myself. I have to say, he is very reliable and the kids love him. We're just friends and after all, he is the girls' birth dad. It's only right that he spends time with them. They are delighted having him in their lives. But, if you came back into my life, I would need time to learn to trust you again. You abused my deepest trust in you and hurt me very much; I might not be able to trust you like that again."

She felt Tom's eyes on her and was careful to not smile and show the feeling of joy, slowly warming her. She looked up and drew her fingers through her shoulder-long blond hair with her right hand, facing him. He had a broad grin on his face, looking rather boyish.

"Bernice, do you still love me?" He definitively looked like a hopeful boy now, his eyes steadily watching her responses. She couldn't help letting a deep sigh escape and a frown appeared.

"I once loved you unconditionally, and you threw it away. I'm not sure what I feel now for you. Of course, you are my children's father and always will be, and you've been a good father to Abby and Shayla, too. But, I realized it was just me who wanted the girls and you just agreed, to please me. I can't hold that against you. I've accepted that I might have to raise them alone as a consequence of my decisions. On the other hand, I wanted you to be able to speak your mind openly and honestly, even if I didn't like what I'm hearing."

She watched his response rather than listened to his words. His face looked rather unconcerned with an expression that was almost happy, she thought.

"Well, that sounds fair. I appreciate your honesty. I'll try to be more honest from now on, I promise. You hurt me too, although I can't blame you for sending that private dick after me. I've got to admit, that was a smart move of you; I'm not sure how long it would have gone on with Marla, and all that time I'd have had to lie to you. In a way, you made it easier for me to move in with her." Tom smiled again.

Bernice straighten up and moved to the edge of her chair with a fierce look in her eyes.

"What are you saying, it's my fault?" Her heart was thumping in her chest while she looked at him, arranging her face, so it wouldn't show her anger.

He rubbed his greying hair back with his right hand, before he replied. Tom's voice had a shade of guilt in it. "No, I'm not blaming you; it's my own fault. I guess that's what people call a mid-life crisis. Well, I'm over it now. My goal was just always to get along, rather than cause a conflict. But, I know that I'm often quiet when I should speak up. I want you to know that I never stopped loving you. It was horrible to lose you and the kids. With Marla it was an ego thing and the sex didn't make up for missing my family. I was a stupid ass." He changed his seat and sat beside her now, inching closer, about to grab her hand.

"Are you saying our sex was lousy?" Sitting with a straight back, her eyes shot killing glances at him. Not the time to take her hand.

"No, I'm not. Nothing was wrong with our sex life, and, since we're going to be honest with each other, it was just maybe a bit subdued. We could spice it up and work on that when we make more time for each other, be alone more often. With Marla, that enhanced my ego, really rather self-centered, I realize that now. After the first shine was gone, there wasn't much left between us."

"Whoa," is all Bernice could say. They sat in silence for a while, sipping their drinks, each checking all of their options in warp speed, their neurons afire. Each following their own train of thoughts.

Bernice realized that she'd just about reached the stage of actually getting over Tom and was prepared to let him go. His question forced her to look at her options. She liked her life as it had unfolded the least half year, with the extra help from Gabriel for the children, and from Tom taking the boys to their activities. She'd been looking at Gabriel with different eyes lately – an attractive man and sincere, although not the most intelligent man she'd ever met.

The real question was whether she could ever trust Tom again, or would she constantly listen for secret calls and conversations cut off in mid-sentence? Would she feel a compulsion to check his e-mail when he wasn't at home? She would have to know his password. Would they still have enough in common as a couple to make it last? His revelations bothered her and the earlier excitement of getting closer to Tom dissipated. What would be the benefits for the kids of reuniting with Tom?

Tom interrupted her train of thought when he touched her lightly on her arm; Bernice didn't withdraw from his touch and she saw he was observing her closely. "How are Beth and Katie?"

"Good, fine. I'm very glad they are my friends; they were good to me, but I do miss socializing with our other friends. I seem to be out of the loop, not invited anymore to the parties, now that I'm single. Kate and Beth seemed the only couple left that didn't feel threatened by my status, although Angela is also still inviting me. I was beginning to think our coupled friends are afraid I'll snatch away their husbands. Did you and Marla get invited to our old friends?"

She knew they had not. Although she wasn't invited anymore to their parties, the women's gossip network was still functional. Sitting next to her straight backed, she saw him slump in his seat when he replied.

"No, not really. They're angry with me for breaking up our marriage. When I bump into any of them, they try to avoid me, even cross the road when they see me first. Maybe the women are thinking infidelity might rub off on their husbands." He laughed, but wasn't sounding happy. Bernice had to laugh; a bit of the old bond they had together in their marriage returned: Making fun of other couples – together against the rest of the world.

Suddenly, she felt tired, even exhausted having to face her future, with all of the problems she still anticipated. Jonathan was only nine. She had at least ten more years of parenting ahead of her, until she could rest and start living just for herself.

"My job hasn't been easy lately with the massive reorganization, and all staff needing to be retrained for the new mission with a 180 degree turn on the teeter-totter of family preservation versus child protection. The new digital transformation is another big thing and the management has no mercy with older workers. I was thinking of changing jobs, or else start working part-time in a job share, if I could get one of the few positions." What she didn't say was she could financially manage on her own with the subsidy from Tom's maintenance payments.

"Sorry to hear that. With my sales picking up lately, that really would be an option, Bernie, if we reconciled. Think about it."

She softly put her hand on his knee and watched him, trying his patience. She saw him shuffling his feet every few seconds, back and forth, trying to find a position that felt more comfortable. Bernice was taking her time to decide.

CHAPTER 29

Had he actually gone too far this time? Tom looked intently at Bernice and studied her face. For a 40-year-old, she was looking good, no gray in her blond hair, hardly any lines in her face, while his hair was pretty gray already. His girth not quite as lean as before, while she had stayed slim. She carried herself well and had a sophisticated style all her own, always the consummate professional dressed in smart clothes and high heels, with great hair that flowed softly around her lovely face. He felt warm; a desire to kiss her crept over him. His heart skipped a beat and he felt turned on, still looking at her, when he suddenly switched his focus, not wanting to be caught staring at her.

Was it because he couldn't have her that the old feelings returned? They used to be good together and he hoped it was possible to blow life into the smoldering embers of their sex life. He glanced around the room and saw mostly couples, with the exception of a group in the bar area on stools. He and Bernice were older than most patrons.

Sure, Bernice was not fresh-faced and young Marla with tight skin and a marvelous body, but he found out that the body was just that: a body. He had to agree with whomever said it first: The most important sex organ was the brain. In hindsight, Marla's obvious ennui with his attempts to have sex had fairly quickly cooled off his amorous heart after moving in with her. If he was honest, within a few weeks the irritation had already set in, with Marla's endless running to the tanning bed, the beauty shop, and the shopping sprees.

Right from the start, Marla had let him always pay her bills. He quickly got the sense she wasn't even interested in what he really thought, or what he was like as a person. She never asked his opinion about anything, other than her new shoes or her hairdo. When he proposed that she'd join him in some of the things he liked, golfing, hiking, and skiing, she'd made a face and came up with all kinds of excuses. Her favourite activities were dining out, watching movies, and hanging out at the bar. When they went out together with her friends, he felt like a sugar daddy. Oh, well, that was her youth. He had made the right decision to end it.

His mind turned toward his children, anticipating playing games and going out together as a family again. He'd have to be home more often and make an effort doing housework as well, maybe even start suppers. This time, he would make sure that his presence at home would be noticed – if she'd let him. He was quite sure Bernice would take him back, as raising four kids alone had never been an option.

Bernice's voice brought him back to the present and he sat up straight. Independently from each other, they seemed to have had their own little thought process along similar pathways.

"Well, what can I tell you, Tom," Bernice said at the right time while putting her hand on his knee. She waved at the waitress with her other hand. Before the woman arrived, she quickly said: "I haven't decided yet, but I'll tell you that I am leaning towards a "yes". I want to talk with a few people and I want you to think about changes that we would need to make. I will come up with some conditions as well."

Happily, and rather disingenuously, he replied. "Really? I thought you were going to reject me. I wouldn't blame you if you did. I'll think about what you said and get something of a proposal on paper. I'm really pleased. Do you want to get a bite to eat now? By the way, who's babysitting?"

They ordered their meals and happily chatted about the kids along a very familiar groove. Bernice expressed her anxiety about Shayla and praised Gabriel in his efforts to help her, stepping up to his responsibilities, and putting in a tremendous effort with the children: "All of them, not just the girls."

Tom reached out, grabbed Bernice's hand, and pressed for a few seconds before letting go. She let him and smiled. He touched her face for a few seconds, stroking her cheek. She grabbed his hand, opened his palm and softly pressed a quick kiss inside his palm before she released it.

His heart flooded with love and the belief formed in him that the bond that seemed lost forever, might be salvageable. He realized that they would look like a happily married couple to any observing outsider. Life does offer second chances to those who can see.